George Gunton

Trusts and the Public

George Gunton

Trusts and the Public

ISBN/EAN: 9783337368272

Printed in Europe, USA, Canada, Australia, Japan

Cover: Foto ©Andreas Hilbeck / pixelio.de

More available books at **www.hansebooks.com**

TRUSTS AND

THE PUBLIC

BY

GEORGE GUNTON

AUTHOR OF "WEALTH AND PROGRESS," "PRINCIPLES OF
SOCIAL ECONOMICS," ETC.

NEW YORK
D. APPLETON AND COMPANY
1899

PREFACE

THIS volume is not a treatise on trusts, but a collection of articles and addresses previously published, discussing the different aspects of the subject as they have arisen during the last twelve years. The first one appeared in 1887 as a series of editorials in the New York *Commercial Bulletin*, now the *Journal of Commerce and Commercial Bulletin*, and was published in revised form in the *Political Science Quarterly*, issued by Columbia University, for September, 1888. This was really about the first attempt seriously to discuss the trust question in its economic and social aspects. It was followed in the next issue of the *Quarterly* by an exhaustive article on the legal aspects of trusts, by Judge Theodore W. Dwight, then the head of the Columbia Law School. From that time on the subject has grown and attracted more and more of public attention, until it has now become an absorbing topic of public discussion.

During this period I have also discussed the subject in the *Social Economist*, its successor *Gunton's Magazine*, the New York *Independent*, and in various public addresses. The editions of the periodicals containing these essays and addresses have in many instances been exhausted, so that several of them are now out of print. The demand for these has become so urgent that it has been deemed advisable to republish a number of them, covering the chief points of the controversy, in a single volume. Of the seventeen articles here reprinted, two, "Trusts *versus* the Town" and "Powers and Perils of the New Trusts," are by Mr. Hayes Robbins, associate editor of *Gunton's Magazine.*

All the articles and addresses appeared at different times; they are really separate papers, and, while they respectively discussed the different phases of the subject as they arose in public controversy, they not infrequently cover the same points; so that, when brought together in this way, there is some repetition. But this was unavoidable without re-writing the whole matter and making the book into a logically connected treatise, which is exactly what it is not intended to be. In view of this fact it was deemed advisable not to revise them and bring the data down to date, but to publish each essay as it appeared and add footnotes referring to the chapters where more recent facts are presented, thus permitting the articles to retain their chronological appropriateness. While from a literary point of view the repetition of facts and arguments is a defect, it may possibly have the merit of serving to emphasize some of the more important points in the controversy.

About every phase of the trust question is discussed in these essays, and, while in the main the principle of trusts as an economic development is defended, the abuses of the trust principle are pointed out and criticised with equal frankness.

In many chapters reference is made to the Standard Oil Company, for the reason that this corporation has constantly been under fire. Nearly all the opposition to trusts is fortified by charges against that

concern.   It has been the subject of legislation in
several states and of high-handed attempts at wholesale blackmail, as well as special pleadings before
the Interstate Commerce Commission and various investigating commissions of congress and the different
states.   Its affairs have been conspicuous in all the
literature of the subject, and therefore necessarily come
up for frequent discussion.

While this little book has the disadvantages necessarily connected with collections of separate essays on
the same subject, it is hoped that its existence will be
justified by the amount of important data it presents,
not elsewhere published in convenient form.

NEW YORK, *October*, 1899.

CONTENTS

THE ECONOMIC AND SOCIAL ASPECTS OF TRUSTS *

" What shall we do with trusts ? " has of late become an absorbing theme of public discussion.   Indeed, the public mind has begun to assume a state of apprehension, almost amounting to alarm, regarding the evil economic and social tendencies of these organizations. Nor is this apprehension limited to professional agitators and chronic alarmists.   It is shared in by all classes. Our foremost journalists, essayists, orators and publicists unite in warning us against the evil consequences to be expected from the organization of trusts, syndicates and the like.   In fact, the social atmosphere seems to be surcharged with an indefinite and almost inexpressible fear of trusts.

In the present state of the public mind upon the subject, to raise a hand against trusts is, *a priori*, a righteous act.   It practically constitutes a standing invitation to politicians,—who, though unfamiliar with economic principles, are very sensitive to public favors,— to enact all sorts of arbitrary laws restricting industrial enterprise, on the principle that to injure a trust is to

---

* Published in the *Political Science Quarterly* of September 1888.

perform a public service. To such an extent is this true that, in one form or another, the proposition to limit these organizations by law has been discussed in both national and state legislatures. Commissions of investigation have been appointed and in some instances restrictive legislation has already been adopted. In obedience to this feeling, one of the great political parties has actually made opposition to trusts a national issue. The interests of industrial and social freedom demand that a truce be called ; at least, until we ascertain whether we are really engaging a public enemy or simply pursuing an industrial phantom. In order to do this, it is necessary carefully to consider what the economic and social aspects of trusts are.

At the outset, it is important clearly to distinguish between the economic character of the organizations and the personal character of the individuals conducting them, because the evils arising from the one require an entirely different kind of treatment from that applied to those caused by the other. If a grocer gives light weight, if he puts sand in his sugar, or peas in his coffee, or if a merchant sells mixed goods for all wool, —that would hardly be a justification for suppressing grocery stores and dry goods houses. In considering the economic and social aspects of trusts, we are not concerned with the personal character of Jay Gould, or the president of the Standard Oil trust, or any manager of great railroad syndicates, but only with the necessary economic and social tendency of the enterprises over which they preside.

The first step in the inquiry is to ascertain what constitutes the distinguishing economic characteristic of trusts. In what, for instance, do they differ, as indus-

trial institutions, from corporations, individual capitalists, or even from hand workers? The more closely
we examine the subject the more clearly we shall see
that they are all fundamentally the same; that the difference is not one of principle, but solely of size and
complexity of industrial organization. The hand laborer
organizes industry on a very simple basis, and on a small
scale. His own personal energy and a few primitive
tools are the only means he is capable of employing.
The individual capitalist or *entrepreneur* differs from
the hand laborer in that he organizes industry on a more
complex basis, and on a larger scale. Instead of being
confined to his own personal energy and such tools as
he himself is capable of using, he employs a number of
individuals together, divides and specializes their labor,
and uses it in conjunction with steam-driven machinery.
The corporation differs from the individual capitalist in
that it consists of the association of a number of capitalists, who, by a greater concentration of capital, are
enabled to organize industry on a still more complex
and extensive basis. And similarly, trusts, which are
the latest form of industrial phenomena, differ from
the corporation in that, instead of being composed of
individual capitalists, they comprise corporations,
which, through a still greater concentration of capital,
make a more minute differentiation and a higher integration of industrial energy possible. The economic
difference between the trust and the corporation, and
that between the corporation and the individual capitalist, is not that one is an aggregation of corporations,
another of individuals, and the third a single individual;
but, like the difference between the hand laborer and
the individual capitalist, it consists entirely in the fact

that one represents a greater aggregation and concentration of capital than the other.

Manifestly, then, the distinguishing economic characteristic of trusts consists of the maximum concentration of capital in productive industry. Therefore the real question involved in considering the economic and social aspects of trusts is: Does the concentration of capital in productive enterprise, whether under trusts, syndicates, or otherwise, necessarily involve economic or social disadvantage to the community? The popular answer to this question is an emphatic, yes! Among the numerous charges upon which trusts and kindred organizations are indicted as public evils are the following:

(1) That they tend to build up monopolies and drive small capitalists out of business;

(2) That they destroy competition, the great minimizer of profits and equalizer of prices;

(3) That they amass fortunes at the expense of the community by increasing the price of commodities;

(4) That they tend to build up an oligarchy which controls legislation in its own interest against that of the community, thereby undermining personal and political freedom, and endangering the existence of democratic institutions.

If these are the necessary results of trusts, it is clearly the duty of the public to check their development. Before taking any steps in that direction, however, it is highly important to ascertain whether these charges are true, and, if true, whether they are the inevitable result of such organizations.

First: Is it true that the concentration of capital tends to build up monopolies? Much here depends upon what is understood by the term monopoly. If by monopoly is meant merely the exclusive power to produce a commodity, this exclusive power may be either an evil or a great benefit, depending entirely upon the way it is obtained. If it is procured through the arbitrary exclusion of competitors, it will surely be an evil; but if derived from the capacity to make the article more cheaply than others, through the use of large capital and superior methods, then it is a positive advantage to the community. It is true that every such advantage is gained by underselling competitors and driving small capitalists from the market; but that, too, is an economic advantage. To understand this it is necessary to remember that there are two kinds of wealth, consumable wealth and productive wealth or capital. The former is wholly devoted to the direct gratification of personal and social wants, while the latter serves no other purpose than that of aiding in the production of more wealth. The sole function of capital is that of a tool. As tools are of no advantage either to their owners or to the public except as they are successfully used in producing wealth, it follows that the only economic and social interest the community can possibly have in either the diffusion or concentration of capital (tools) is that it shall be so employed as to produce consumable wealth most cheaply.

The income of the capitalist class consists of profits, which the community is not interested either in sustaining or increasing. On the contrary, it is always interested in minimizing the proportion of the product which goes to the capitalist as profits, and maximizing that which goes to the community in low prices and high wages. Clearly, therefore, society can have no interest in sustaining the small capitalist unless he can produce wealth as cheaply as the large one; any more than a manufacturer has in sustaining a lazy, incompetent workman in preference to an efficient one. The public could better afford to pension small manufacturers as paupers than to pay the high prices resulting inevitably from the inferior methods their limited capital can employ. Nor is this necessarily a disadvantage to the discharged capitalist, because the large, and hence successful, capitalist can give him employment as a manager or overseer at a higher salary than he could obtain as an isolated small manufacturer; and this is what has occurred wherever industrial integration has taken place on any considerable scale. Strictly speaking, the concentration of capital does not drive small capitalists out of business, but simply integrates them into a larger and more complex system of production, in which they are enabled to produce wealth more cheaply for the community and obtain a larger income for themselves. Consequently, the economic absorption of small capitalists by large ones, instead of being a public evil, is a public advantage, because it can only take place when it serves the community better.

Second: The next charge is that the concentration of capital tends to destroy competition. This is a serious mistake. When the products of the small factory undersold those of the hand-loom and drove the hand-loom weaver out of the market, it did not destroy competition. It is true, competition ceased between the factory and the hand-loom weaver, but it immediately commenced between small manufacturers. Hence, instead of destroying competition, it only changed the plane upon which the competition took place. Again, when competition began between small manufacturers, it was much fiercer than ever it had been between hand-loom weavers. The same was true when small manufacturers began to integrate into corporations. The products of the corporation undersold those of the small manufacturer, and practically drove him from the market; but that did not destroy competition, for, when the small manufacturer ceased to compete with the large corporation, another corporation took his place, and competition was raised to a still higher plane; that is, to a plane between stronger contestants, in which the competition was necessarily more severe. What was true of the hand-loom weaver and small manufacturer, and the small manufacturer and the corporation, is now true of trusts. By the use of large capital, improved machinery and better facilities, the trust can and does undersell the corporation; but that is not destroying competition. It is simply making trusts necessary in all large industries, and thus again raising the plane of competition, from the domain of corporations to that of trusts.[1] The competition between trusts naturally tends to reduce the profits to a closer margin than did the competition between corporations, for the reason that the larger the business transacted the smaller the percentage of profit necessary to its success. Thus, instead of the concentration of capital tending to destroy competition

---

[1] Witness the organizations of the sugar warehouse men, the tin and copper manufacturers, the millers, the farmers and fruit growers, all of which have been made necessary by the severe competition caused by large concerns which can do the business at the minimum cost.

and encourage large profits, the reverse is true. It tends to raise the plane and increase the intensity of competition, and minimize the margin of profits.

Third: The third complaint is that the concentration of capital tends to increase prices. This is the most important charge of all. Whatever the advantage derived from the concentration of capital in productive industry may be, if it tends to increase the prices of commodities, that would be an evil sufficient to warrant its arrest; and as the whole history of industrial progress has been in the direction of the concentration of capital into larger and larger establishments, it would prove, if the charge be true, that the industrial development of modern civilization is on the wrong track, and nothing short of revolution could redeem us from its evil effects.

Fortunately for civilization, all the facts of industrial history point the other way. It is a well-established principle, both in economics and practical business, that capital is most effective in producing consumable wealth where it is most concentrated. The modern factory and railroad systems, which have done so much to cheapen wealth and increase the comfort and convenience of society during the present century, would have been absolutely impossible upon any other principle than that of colossal aggregation of capital.

That the concentration of capital into large enterprises is an economic and social advantage, tending to increase production, to lower prices, and to raise wages, is demonstrated in the history of every progressive country and every successful manufacturing establishment in the world. In short, the use of large capital, the specialization of labor, and the concentration of productive power are the infallible evidence, not only that wealth is being more economically and abundantly produced, but that the community in general, and the wage-receivers in particular, are obtaining a constantly increasing proportion of the product. Large establishments sustain the same economic relation to small ones that steam and electricity sustain to hand labor. The railroad supplanted the pack-horse and stage coach for no other reason than that it served the community better. When the small farm or factory is driven from the field by the larger one, it is always because the latter does the work better and cheaper than the former. As an illustration of this principle, let us take the progress in the cotton industry in the United States since 1830. In that industry, according to the United States census for 1880, the investment of capital, the number of establishments, amount and price of product, and wages paid in 1830 and 1880 were as follows:

	1830	1880
Number of establishments	801	756
Aggregate capital invested	$40,612,984	$208,280,346
Number of lbs. cloth produced	59,514,926	607,264,241
Number of persons employed	62,208	172,544
Number of spindles employed	1,246,703	10,653,435
Amount of capital to establishment	$50,702	$275,503
Ratio of lbs. produced to capital	1.4 to $1.00	2.4 to $1.00
Ratio of capital to persons employed	$652.85 to 1	$1207.17 to 1

[1 The census of 1890 showed, for the cotton industry : Number of establishments 905 ; total capital invested $354,020,843 ; average capital to establishment $391,183 ; persons employed 218,876 ; number of spindles 14,188,103 ; average weekly wages of men operatives $7.62, of women $5.44 ; value of products $267,981,-724 ; per capita consumption of raw cotton 18 lbs., (this in 1880 was 15 lbs.). The price of sheetings per yard, August 1890, is 4¼ cents.]

	1830	1880
Ratio of spindles to persons employed	22 to 1	62 to 1
Ratio of capital to spindles employed	$32.58 to 1	$19.55 to 1
Ratio of lbs. produced to persons employed, ...	950.7 to 1	3519.5 to 1
Ratio of lbs. produced to spindles .	47.6 to 1	57.0 to 1
Annual consumption of lbs. of cotton cloth per capita	5.90	13.91
Price of cotton cloth per yard [sheetings]	17 cts.	7 cts.
Operative's wages per week [1] . . .	$2.55	$5.40

It will thus be seen that in the 756 large establishments in 1880, in which the aggregate capital invested was five times as great as that in 801 small establishments in 1830, the capital invested per spindle was one-third less, the number of spindles operated by each laborer nearly three times as large, the product per spindle one-fourth greater, the product per dollar invested twice as large, the price of the cotton cloth nearly sixty per cent. less, the consumption per capita of the population over one hundred per cent. greater, and wages more than double. What is true of this industry is true of all industries where the concentration of capital has taken place.

It may be urged that the cotton industry has never been under the control of a trust or syndicate, and that the evil effects of concentration do not begin until the trust period is reached. Among the most formidable concentrations of capital which have come under the unfortunate name of trusts or syndicates are those

---

[1] These are women's wages. I have taken the wages of women because there were not men enough employed as cotton operatives in 1830 to warrant a fair comparison; but to the extent that they were so employed their wages have risen in a similar ratio to those of women.

devoted to railroading, telegraphing, and the production of petroleum. There are others of similar proportions, but these stand as the monster evils most to be feared in this country. And, furthermore, these trusts have been in existence the longest, and the true economic tendency of such organizations will therefore be most clearly indicated in their history. What are the facts in relation to these?

We will take, first, petroleum. Not only is the production of petroleum in the hands of a trust, but it is probably the largest trust in the world. The worst of these evils, therefore, may be expected to be found in the history of the Standard Oil Company; and if there are any special advantages in trusts we may expect to find there the best results also.

There are, now, several economic advantages in connection with these institutions that are not to be found in individual corporations. When corporations were isolated they were in competition with each other, not only in the selling market, but in the productive process also, and each one who discovered an improvement in the manufacture naturally took special pains to keep it from all competitors. Under trust companies this is reversed. No sooner is an improvement found by any one corporation, than it is, from common interest, applied to all; hence the economy which was previously confined to a single corporation now becomes a part of the process of the whole product in the market, —at least, so far as the trust is concerned. Again when corporations combine they are enabled to manufacture all their own supplies on the largest possible scale, and are thereby enabled to employ the most improved methods of production in every department.

This is exactly what has been accomplished by trusts.
For example, before the organization of the Standard
Oil Company in 1872, oil had to be transported from
the wells to the market by the railroads in small
quantities, in barrels, tanks, etc. After the organization of that company, these various methods were
superseded by one general pipe line, which takes the
oil directly from the well to the market. There are
two such lines reaching New York, with a capacity of
25,000 barrels per day. There is also one such line to
Philadelphia, one to Baltimore, another to Buffalo,
another to Cleveland, and another to Pittsburg, and
one is now being laid to Chicago. This was an under-
taking absolutely impracticable for any of the smaller
corporations. The result is a saving of 66⅔ per cent.
on the cost of transportation alone. In 1872 it cost
$1.50 to transport a barrel of oil to New York; to-day
it costs only 50 cents. In 1872, barrels cost $2.35
each; to-day the Standard Oil trust manufactures
them for its own use at $1.25 each, a reduction of 47
per cent., or a saving of nearly $4,000,000 a year. In
the cost of the manufacture of tin cans, a saving of 50
per cent. has been made, the price having been reduced
from 30 to 15 cents per can since 1874. As this company uses about 30,000,000 tin cans a year, that makes
a saving of over $4,500,000 annually. The same is
true of wooden cases, which in 1874 cost 20 cents each.
The company now manufactures them for itself at a
cost of 13 cents each, being an annual saving of about
$1,250,000.

Who was benefited by all this economy, is the
question that naturally arises in this connection. Did
it go into the pockets of the Standard Oil Company as

profits, or did it accrue to the community in the reduced price of oil? That question can best be answered by the facts, as shown in the following table : [1]

Year	Shipments from wells. Bbl.	Stock of crude oil on hand. Bbl.	Price of crude oil per gallon at wells.	Price per gallon of refined oil for export.
1871	5,667,891	568,858	10.52 cts.	24.24 cts.
1872	5,890,942	1,174,000	9.43	23.75
1873	9,499,775	1,625,157	4.12	18.21
1874	8,821,500	3,705,639	2.81	13.09
1875	8,924,938	2,751,758	2.96	12.99
1876	9,583,949	1,926,735	5.99	19.12
1877	12,496,644	2,857,098	5.08	15.92
1878	13,750,090	4,307,590	2.76	10.87
1879	16,226,586	8,094,496	2.09	8.08
1880	15,839,020	16,606,344	2.24	9.12
1881	19,340,021	25,333,411	2.30	8.05
1882	22,094,209	34,335,174	1.87	7.41
1883	21,967,636	35,715,565	2.52	8.14
1884	24,053,902	36,872,892	1.99	8.28
1885	24,029,424	33,836,930	2.11	7.86
1886	26,332,445	33,395,885	1.69	7.07
1887	26,627,191	28,310,282	1.59	6.75

It will be seen by the above that from 1871, the year before the Standard Oil Company was organized, to 1878, the year before the pipe line was laid, the price of refined oil fell 13.37 cents per gallon. From the laying of the pipe line to the organization of the trust in 1881 it fell 2.82 cents per gallon, and from the organization of the trust to 1887 it fell 1.30 cents per gallon. Thus, through the economies introduced into the production and transportation of petroleum since 1871, the price of refined oil has been reduced 17.49 cents per

---

[1] See New York Produce-Exchange Reports, 1873–4, p. 483 ; 1875–6, p. 445 ; 1876–7, p. 405 ; 1882, p. 773. Also New York Chamber of Commerce Reports for 1869–70, p. 45 ; 1871–2, p. 54 ; 1875–6, p. 50 ; 1878–9, p. 98 ; 1882–3, p. 67 ; 1886–7, p. 65 ; 1887–8, p. 73.

gallon, or 72 per cent., being a saving to the consumers of the 998,953,011 gallons of refined oil used last year alone of $174,716,881.[1]

It may be said that this great fall in the price is partly the result of the fall in price of crude oil. That is true, but much of this fall is also due to the improved facilities applied at the wells by this company. But were it true that this reduction is all attributable to causes over which the Standard Oil trust has no control, which is absurd, that cannot be said of the fall in the price of refined oil in excess of that of the crude. It will be seen from the table quoted above, that since 1871 the price of crude oil has fallen 8.93 cents per gallon, leaving a net fall in the price of refined oil, over and above that of the crude, of 8.56 cents per gallon, or 1.81 cents per gallon more than the total price now paid for it. This reduction in price is due exclusively to the improved methods introduced into the various processes of refining and transporting oil. If the price of refined oil had only fallen in the same ratio as that of crude, it would to-day cost the consumer 15.30 cents per gallon instead of 6.75 cents, the price at which it was sold in 1887. It will thus be seen that, giving the opposition the full benefit of all the doubts, the consumers of refined oil in 1887 had a clear gain of $85,410,482, as the result of the efforts of the Standard Oil Company; and still we are told that trusts tend to advance prices to the consumer.

Another trust company that has been singled out for censure is the one engaged in the manufacture of cot-

[1 For more complete and recent data of oil production and prices see "Crusade against Prosperity," the sixteenth paper in this volume.]

ton-seed oil. So strong is the feeling against trusts, that an effort has recently been made to impose a tax upon the product of this company, not to make it reduce, but to force it to increase the price of its product, in order that hog-fat manufacturers might have a special advantage. Notwithstanding this opposition, the price of cotton-seed oil has fallen, along with the economic improvement in its production introduced by the trust. In 1878 the average price of standard summer yellow oil was 47.94 cents per gallon. In 1883, the year before the organization of the trust, it had only fallen to 47.08 cents per gallon. In 1887, four years after the organization of the trust, it had fallen to 38.83 cents per gallon.[1] In other words, during these four years the price of cotton-seed oil fell more than eight times as much as it did during the five years before the trust was formed.[2]

What is true of petroleum and cotton-seed oil is also true of sugar and other products. Although the sugar trust has not been organized long enough to give any specific results, the concentration of capital in that industry has been steadily increasing for years, and the prices show a commensurate tendency downward. In 1880, the price of " Grocers' Standard A White Sugar " was $9.48½ per barrel. It has continued to fall every year since that date, until in 1887 it was only $5.66[3]

---

[1] These facts are taken from the prices quoted in the market reports of the *New York Daily Commercial Bulletin* on the first of every month from January 1878 to December, 1887.

[2 The price of cotton-seed oil is now, August 1899, 25 cents per gallon.]

[3] See New York Chamber of Commerce Reports for 1880–1, p. 17 ; 1882–3, p. 18 ; 1883–4, p. 18 ; 1884–5, p. 18 ; 1885–6, p. 18 ; 1886–7, p. 18 ; 1887–8, p. 18.

per barrel, and other grades of sugar and molasses have fallen in a similar and some in even a greater ratio.[1]

Another of the large organizations against which the hardest things are said is the railroad syndicate. We hear a great deal about railroad monopolies and their robbery of the public by the high rates made possible by these colossal combinations. An examination of the freight tariffs on the trunk lines shows the same general reduction in prices that we have seen in the case of the Standard Oil and other trusts. The average rates for sending a hundred pounds of freight from New York to Chicago in 1862 and in 1888 were as follows, showing a reduction of 51 per cent.:

	1862	1888
First class	$1.63	$0.75
Second class	1.32	.65
Third class	1.05	.50
Fourth class	.66	.35

It may be added that the rates for the second and third classes have each been advanced five cents per hundred pounds, through the beneficial influence of the interstate commerce law.

Another formidable organization that has afforded a theme for considerable moralizing is that of the telegraph system. The Western Union Telegraph Company is, perhaps, next to the Standard Oil trust, regarded as the worst monopoly in this country. It is well known that, prior to 1866, our telegraphic service was done through a host of small local companies. To

[1 At the time this article was published, September 1888, the price of granulated sugar was 7¼ cents per pound. It is now, August 1899, 5¼ cents.]

send a message across the country involved its going through the hands of not less than half a dozen companies. In 1866 these were integrated into one organization under the name of the Western Union Telegraph Company.

Since the concentration of capital in the telegraphic service under this organization, the rates for messages from New York to the large centers throughout the country have been reduced 85 per cent., as is shown by the following table:

Rates for sending ten words from New York:

	1866	1888		1866	1888
To Chicago . .	$2.20	$0.40	To Minneapolis [1] . .	$2.10	$0.60
" St. Louis . .	2.55	.40	" Buffalo . . .	.75	.25
" St. Paul . .	2.25	.50	" Wash'gton, D. C.	.75	.25
" Cincinnati .	1.99	.40	" San Francisco .	7.45	1.00
" New Orleans	3.25	.60	" Oregon	10.20	1.00
" Galveston .	5.50	.75	" W. Territory .	12.00	1.00

Moreover, in 1868, when this company sent only 6,404,595 messages, it cost the company, on an average, 63.4 cents per message; and, in order to make a profit on the capital invested, the average price charged to the community was $1.047 per message, leaving 41.3 cents profit per message. In 1887, when the company sent 47,394,530 messages, the average cost per message was 23 cents; and the average toll to the community was reduced to 30.4 cents per message, leaving only 7.4 cents profit per message.[2] It will thus be seen that during the twenty years of this " monopoly " the aver-

---

[1 The rate to Minneapolis is now (1899) 50 cents.]

[2] The average cost per message in 1897–98 was 24.7 cents. and the average toll to the public 20.1 cents per message, leaving a profit of 5.4 cents.

age cost of messages to the community, to all points, has been reduced 74.3 cents per message, or over 70 per cent.; and that the profits have been reduced 33 cents per message. In other words, the total cost of the service to the community to-day is 10.9 cents per message less than the profits alone were before the organization of this company.

It may perhaps be said that, although these trusts have constantly resulted in reducing prices, should the government run the business a still greater saving would be accomplished. This idea has been so extensively and favorably received that the demand for government ownership of railroads and telegraphs has become one of the stock resolutions in all industrial reform movements, and the proposition for the government to take possession of the telegraph lines is actually before Congress in a bill introduced in the Senate.

There are many reasons why this, in the nature of things, would not be an improvement. Arbitrary monopoly is the natural harbinger of irresponsibility, incompetency and waste, and hence naturally tends to give inferior products at maximum prices. While this is true of all artificial monopoly, it is especially true of government monopoly. The head of a government enterprise, having no interest in the profit, has no necessary incentive for developing improved methods of service. On the contrary, he has a direct interest in keeping the number of employees at the maximum, because, by the disposition of industrial favors, he can command political allegiance, which is the power he chiefly relies upon to retain his position. And this tendency is strongest under democratic institutions, because it is there that the political potency of the laborer is the greatest. Under a system where political influence, rather than economic efficiency, is thus the condition of employment, and where there is little responsibility and no redress for the injury and loss caused by delay and blunders through incapacity, poor or at best mediocre service must necessarily result.

Nor is this mere speculation, for extensive experiments in government telegraphy have already been tried, and the facts speak for themselves. In all European countries the telegraphic service is in the hands of the state. We therefore have ample opportunities for testing the matter by experience. It should be noted here, that under private enterprise in this country the company is responsible for losses caused by the failure or delay in delivery, while no such protection is afforded to the interest of the citizens under any existing system of state telegraphy. As under our postal system, the government is entirely irresponsible, at least to the individual with whom it is doing business. If the citizen is utterly ruined by the inefficiency of the department, he has absolutely no redress; he pays his money and takes all the risk.

The most efficient system of state telegraphy in the world, and the one which gives the lowest rates of toll to the public, is that of Great Britain. England possesses exceptionally favorable conditions for giving cheap telegraph service. In many important respects her advantages are superior to ours. She has a limited, thickly settled, well-cleared country, while we have an extensive, sparsely settled, ill-cleared country to operate in. The extreme distance between terminal stations in England does not exceed 600 miles, with (in

1887) 29,895 miles of line, carrying 173,539 miles of wire and cable, with 6,500 offices, and transmitting about 50,000,000 messages per annum.[1] In this country the extreme distance between terminal stations is nearly 5,000 miles, with 176,000 miles of line, carrying 630,000 miles of wire and cable, maintaining 17,000 offices to do the business of 55,000,000 messages.[2]

With such natural advantages over this country, and with wages one-fourth lower, if there is any efficacy in government ownership Great Britain ought to be able to serve the public vastly cheaper than private enterprise in this country can possibly do. Is such the case? Let the facts answer.

The rate of tolls in England since the reduction two years ago is 12 cents for twelve words, including date, address and signature. As the date, address and signature will average from ten to fourteen words, it will cost from 23 cents to 25 cents to send a ten-word despatch, which is but a fraction less than the rate in this country. The press despatches are transmitted much more cheaply here than in England. But even this seeming cheapness in the English service is unreal, for the rate of toll does not represent the price the public actually pays for it; because, with the exception of the first two years of government ownership, the postal telegraph has never paid expenses, as is shown by the following table,[3] the deficiency of course having to be made up out of taxes:

---

[1] In 1897–98 there were 10,483 offices, and about 83,000,000 messages of all descriptions were sent.]

[2] During the year 1897–98 the Western Union Telegraph Company maintained 22,210 offices, forwarded 62,173,749 messages, and operated 189,847 miles of line, carrying 874,420 miles of wire.]

[3] Parliamentary Reports on Postal Telegraph, 1886–87.

Postal Telegraph Deficiencies in England.[1]

1872	. . $771,036.82	1880	. . $143,563.78
1873	. . 854,335.12	1881	. . 4,772.94
1874	. . 997,910.50	1882	. . 540,166.04
1875–76	. 919,842.00	1883	. . 682,672.96
1877	. . 898,843.42	1884	. . 1,661,348.22
1878	. . 907,518.72	1885	. . 1,741,228.50
1879	. . 547,774.18	1886	. . 2,255,232.00

It will be seen from this table that the deficiency in the telegraphic service of Great Britain has averaged nearly a million dollars a year ever since state owner-ship began, and in 1886, the first full year of the present rate, the deficit was over two and a quarter million dollars, to which must be further added about one and a half million dollars for interest on the bonds given for the plant when the government purchased the telegraph in 1870.[1] Thus, in addition to what is directly paid for the service by the consumer, about $7\frac{1}{2}$ cents per message is paid indirectly in taxes, making a total of over 30 cents per message of ten words; while the cost in this country is only 20 cents for ten words in large cities and 25 cents for ten words for distances of four or five hundred miles, the average for all the messages, both long and short, being only 30.4 cents per message.

From these facts it will be seen that with natural disadvantages in this country which make it necessary to cover eight times as much distance between the terminal stations, to have three times as many miles of line, three and a half times as many miles of wire and cable, and to maintain two and a half times as many

[1 The deficit in 1897–98 amounted to $1,504,355 ; or, adding interest on bonds given for the plant, about $3,000,000.]

offices, and with wages much higher, private enterprise can render about the same amount of telegraphic service as cheaply and with more efficiency and despatch than is done by state ownership in England. And, it may be added, that those who do the business here make a living profit, while there they do it for nothing, or run into debt. The proposition to substitute state telegraphy for private enterprise in this country, in the face of such facts, is surely entitled to be designated by some other name than statesmanship.

Those who advocate governmental control of large industries would probably refer us to the management of the post-office, which is always cited as the model experiment in collective ownership. The fact is pointed out that it formerly cost twenty cents to carry a letter across the country while it now costs only two cents, as an evidence of the economic success of the state control. There are few facts which the public accept more implicitly and regard as more conclusive than these; yet there are few more delusive and misleading. It is true that we can now send a letter three thousand miles for two cents, but if we examine the matter a little closer we shall see that this is not due to anything the government has done. All the government does in the postal service is to collect, assort, stamp and bag outgoing, and deliver incoming, letters; give out and receive money orders; and render an account of the business done. No improved methods have been introduced during the last twenty-five years in that part of the postal system which the government controls. Letters are stamped by hand, and delivered and collected by individual messengers, just as they were fifty years ago. All the economy in the postal

service has come from the improved methods of transporting the mail, and this, it should be remembered, is
all done by private enterprise.   From the moment the
letter-bag leaves the door of the post-office it enters the
hands of private enterprise.   It is the great railroads,
steamship companies, etc., and not the government, that
have made it possible for letters to go three thousand
miles for two cents.   Indeed, it is more than probable
that had the postal system been under the control of
private enterprise, instead of that of the state (managed
by mediocre politicians), letters would ere this have
been stamped by machinery and collected from street
boxes by electricity, and that other improvements would
have been introduced which would have sufficiently
economized labor to render one-cent postage possible
without running into debt.

There is still another class of objectors to the concentration of capital in the form of trusts.   These are
sufficiently careful and well informed of the facts to
know that trusts have not, as is commonly asserted, yet
shown any tendency to increase prices.   Their fears,
however, all relate to what may happen in the future,
when the trusts, having organized in all branches of industry, become masters of the situation.   It is not, according to them, until that point of industrial concentration is reached, that the evils of trusts will be upon
us, but when that time comes it will be too late to call
a halt.   The community will then be completely at the
mercy of the colossal capitalists, and we may expect
not only a rise in the price of the necessaries of life,
but all the kindred evils monopoly implies.

This statement has a more plausible seeming than
those which fly in the face of all known facts, but upon

examination it will, I think, be found to be scarcely less erroneous. If the trusts control all the productive processes, it is asked, what is to prevent them from putting prices at whatever height they choose? I answer, that which is to them the most important of all considerations, namely, *self-interest.* If it could be shown that their interest would be promoted by raising prices, I freely confess that there would be little hope of the fact being otherwise. It should always be remembered that capital is one of the most sensitive things in the world ;—it has been well said that nothing is so cowardly as a million dollars, except two million dollars. Capital always shrinks at the sight of losses, and it will run almost any risk for probable profits. Knowing this as no others do, the monopolists, so-called, see very clearly that if they put their prices so high that the margin of profit is abnormal, capital will at once leave other industries and rush into theirs. Capital is ever waiting for just such opportunities. It may be said that if new capital comes into the business they will buy it up. But that takes money, and a million dollars invested in buying up a competitor might, with much more safety, be invested in reducing prices ; because a new competitor may prove too strong to be bought up, in which case the monopolists themselves may be driven from the field or have their profits reduced to the lowest point. They have therefore a direct interest in keeping prices at least sufficiently low not to invite the organization of counter enterprises which may destroy their existing profits. If the gates for the admission of new competitive capital are always open, the economic effect is substantially the same as if the new competitor were already there ; the fact that

he *may come* any day has essentially the same effect as
if he *had come*, because to *keep him out* requires the
same kind of influence that would be necessary to
drive him out.   And, as the latter always involves
greater risks than the former, on the principle of self-
interest the former is most likely to be adopted.[1]
There is really little to fear, in this line, so long as arbitrary barriers are kept out of the way, because in the
absence of legal restrictions the active influence of the
potential competitor is ever present.

Fourth: The next charge against trusts is that,
through their immense wealth, they are obtaining an
increasing control over the government, and are
thereby tending to become not only industrial monopolists but political dictators also, the latter being
the natural consequence of the former.   This charge, I
think, upon investigation will also prove to be unfounded.   Notwithstanding the wholesale complaints
that legislation is all in their interest, the statute books
of the various states show no evidence of this charge.
Instead of laws being enacted to grant special favors
to these corporations, the books bristle with enact-
ments directed against them.   It is true that they have
lobbyists, and perhaps spend large sums of money
during the legislative sessions; but any one who will
investigate the matter will find that it is almost invari-
ably to defeat legislation directed against them, and
not to enact new laws in their favor.   They need no
legislation in their favor.   They are strong enough,

---

[1] This is clearly shown in the history of the Standard Oil Company.   During the last ten years this company has had practically no competitor.   Still the price of oil has steadily tended
downwards.

by virtue of their concentrated capital and improved methods of production, to hold their place in the industrial world.

Instead of growing in political power they are constantly becoming politically ostracized, as is shown by the increasing unpopularity of the presidents and other prominent officials of trust companies. Fifty years ago it would have been regarded as a favor by the community for a rich manufacturer to accept any position. Just in proportion as this industrial concentration and specialization has developed, the political attitude of the community has changed towards capitalistic magnates, until to-day the president of the Standard Oil Company, or of the Western Union Telegraph Company, or of a railroad syndicate, whatever his personal qualifications, could hardly be elected as a member of a board of aldermen. Nor is there anything unjust in this attitude. These men have not developed the qualities of statesmanship. They have developed simply the capacity of industrial managers, and as such, in the specialization of social and economic forces, they naturally gravitate to the field of operation where they are experts. Hence, in proportion as they become industrial specialists, they recede as political leaders. This is also shown by the fact that if they want to affect legislation they are compelled to do it indirectly, because to be known is to be defeated.

But those who take this pessimistic view, when asked for facts, failing to find them in modern experience, generally point us to ancient Rome, and bid us take warning of her fate. They, with considerable eloquence and pathos, remind us that when the wealth of Rome began to be concentrated into a few hands, the people were oppressed, political corruption and private immorality ran rampant, and intellectual, political and national decay set in, which culminated with the destruction of her civilization. To say that because the concentration of wealth led to political and national degeneracy in Rome in the fourth century, the concentration of *capital* will produce the same results in the nineteenth century, is illogical to the last degree. This conclusion is based upon the very common assumption that all concentration of wealth tends to impoverish the masses. That is a fundamental error, which arises from the failure to recognize the distinction between consumable wealth and productive wealth.

It is true that the concentration of consumable wealth in the hands of one class lessens the amount available for the others. But this is not true of the concentration of productive wealth (capital), because, as I have already shown, capital fills no other function than that of a tool; hence no class is the richer for owning capital, except as they obtain the consumable wealth that it produces. Under Rome it was the consumable and not the productive wealth that was concentrated. It is notorious that nothing was held in more contempt in the Roman imperial period than industry. It is said that Augustus pronounced the sentence of death upon Senator Ovinius for " having so degraded himself as to engage in manufacture." Rome was essentially a military and not an industrial state. She lived by plunder rather than production, and her wealth was distributed by authority rather than economic law. Hence the history of Rome, instead of illustrating the necessary consequences of present industrial tendencies, shows, rather, what may naturally be expected from the arbitrary manipulation of industrial affairs.

Since capital is of no use to any one except as it produces enjoyable commodities, and since the capitalist can obtain no enjoyable commodities as the result of concentrated capital except as he can sell its products, it follows that capital can only be advantageous to the *capitalist* when its products are generally and liberally consumed by the community, and, consequently, the concentration of capital is economically possible only in proportion as the consumable wealth it produces is generally distributed. For this reason the arbitrary concentration of consumable wealth in Rome made the concentration of productive wealth impossible, and, conversely, the natural concentration of productive wealth to-day makes the concentration of consumable wealth impossible. It is of the very essence of economic law that consumable wealth is most widely distributed in proportion as productive wealth (capital) is concentrated. Thus, by the same economic law that the social and political degradation of the masses was increased by the concentration of consumable wealth under Rome, their material prosperity and political independence are promoted by the concentration of productive wealth under modern industrial institutions.

Manifestly, therefore, the charge that the concentration of capital in the form of trusts and syndicates necessarily tends to produce monopoly (in the obnoxious sense), destroy competition, increase prices, oppress labor, or to put the government into the hands of an industrial oligarchy, is without any real foundation in fact or justification in reason. On the contrary, these institutions, instead of being the evidence of industrial abnormality and economic disease, are the natural consequence of modern industrial differentiation, and in their nature are economically wholesome, and politically and socially harmless.

In taking this view of the economic and social aspects of trusts, I do not assume the moral sponsorship of all that is done in their name and behalf. I am not unmindful of the fact that many evils have grown up with the development of these organizations, which demand the most serious consideration and vigorous treatment. But I insist that this is not an inseparable part of these institutions, and hence that it is not necessary to check their economic development in order to suppress the moral and social evils that have become associated with them. The corruption of the lobby and the coercion of competitors are no more necessary to trusts than venal voters are to democratic institutions, than mercenary decisions are to the jury system, than blatant demagogy is to free speech, or than superficial, sensational and fawning journalism is to a free press. It is a characteristic feature of all social development that the advent of new and more complex phenomena always creates the possibility of new evils. And it is only to the extent that these evils are eliminated, without impairing the good that any real progress is finally assured. To promote this eliminating process is the function of true statesmanship. In order to do this with any appreciable success we must learn to recognize the important but generally ignored fact that all social, political and moral institutions finally rest upon and are adjusted to and determined by the character of the great mass of the community. It is a well established fact that business immorality and political chicanery are the most general where the social, intellectual and moral character of the masses is the lowest. Hence we always find the habitual misrepresentation of the quality, quantity and price of merchandise, and the systematic packing of caucuses and bribing or coercion of voters, most prevalent among the poorest and most ignorant classes.

Therefore, if we want to improve the character of congressmen, we must elevate that of their constituents, and for the same reason in order to elevate and purify the tone of the press we must improve that of the readers. The only way to prevent the capitalists from corrupting legislation in the lobbies is to increase the integrity of the caucus. Those who buy votes may always be expected to sell legislation. As the evils associated with trusts are mainly ethical in their nature, their elimination should not be sought in any arbitrary limitation of trusts as industrial institutions,[1] but it should be sought in the direction of a more perfect administration of the criminal law and in increas-

---

[1] The present tendency of legislation is strongly in that direction. Since writing the above I have received the full text of a bill recently introduced into congress proposing to levy a tax of 40 per cent on the products of trusts. This measure, which is characteristic of all the proposed legislation upon the subject, is essentially uneconomic in character. Instead of tending to eliminate the bad features of trusts without impairing the good, it would produce the opposite effect. If it did not make the development of large enterprises impossible it would destroy their economic advantages by making their products 40 per cent. dearer to the public.

ing the influences which tend to improve the social condition and develop the intellectual and moral character of the great mass of the people, who constitute the only power that can make such evils impossible. It must not be inferred, however, that the economic phase of trusts and similar organizations is necessarily outside the pale of state action. But if the community is to secure the best economic results from the use of capital and obtain the maximum production at lowest prices, the state should promote rather than restrict the free movement and safe concentration of capital in productive enterprise. One of the ways in which the state can render efficient service in this regard, without interfering in any way with the freedom of capital, would be to furnish frequent, reliable statistics as to the cost of production, including that of raw material, wages and transportation, and also the selling price of the product in large industries. With such statistics, scientifically collected and authoritatively presented, whenever abnormal profits existed in any industry the fact would be generally known; and idle and less remunerative capital would at once move in that direction. By this means the mobility and consequently the competitive influence of capital would be greatly increased, and the full benefits of large enterprises and improved methods of production would be secured to the community by the necessarily minimized prices and profits.

II

THE ECONOMIC ERRORS OF TRUSTS *

Iᴛ has been well said that there is generally "a soul of truth in things erroneous." When historically investigated, the crudest theological, political, and economic superstitions are generally found to have had their rise in some actual experience. The public generally misunderstands and often exaggerates social facts, but it seldom invents them. Whenever public sentiment turns against established institutions, we may be sure that it is not entirely without cause, however irrational the proposed remedies may be. What then is the cause of this popular antagonism to trusts? Is it due to some peculiarity inherent in this form of industrial organization, or does it arise from erroneous ideas of administration? In short, are trusts a legitimate form of economic development, or are they simply a form of monopoly superimposed upon society?

Many people talk about trusts as if they were a sudden creation, the product of a conspiracy against the public. Nothing could be farther from the truth than this view. The history of trusts is simply the history of the continuous and almost imperceptible tendency in progressive society toward a greater centralization of capital which the most highly developed labor-saving methods of production make neces-

---

* Published in the *Social Economist* of February 1893.

sary.   The impeachment of trusts as economic institutions is therefore the impeachment of the concentration of capital, without which, it is needless to say, our great railroad, telegraph, and factory systems would have been impossible.   Very few of the industries which use the most approved methods and have contributed most to cheapening the multitude of products can now be conducted with a capital of less than a million dollars; many of them require tens and even hundreds of millions.   Such large capitals would be absolutely impossible without the cooperation of the great capitalists.   If the evil lies in the amount of capital aggregated in a single concern, then what shall the limit be ?   If a hundred million is dangerous, why not fifty million ?   And if fifty, why not twenty-five, or ten, or even one ?   A hundred or even fifty years ago, a millionaire might have been regarded with as much apprehension as is a hundred-millionaire to-day ; indeed, he would have sustained about the same relation to the productive needs and methods of the community.   The truth is that in this case, as in the growth of all social institutions, the new form came because it was necessary.   The small English water-wheel factory on the river bank, in the eighteenth century, came because the isolated hand-loom and spinning-wheel did not permit the utilization of the most economic methods after the spinning-jenny and spinning-frame were invented.   The steam-driven factory in thickly populated centers came in the first quarter of the nineteenth century because the water-wheel shops were incapable of employing the best methods after the invention of steam and the power-loom had been completed.   If these had not been capable of lessening the cost of production and so rendering a general benefit to the community, they could not have succeeded, as there would have been no demand for their products. So, again, by the middle of the century, when machinery had been still further improved, partnership organization of industry became necessary because single individuals were not rich enough to furnish plants sufficiently large to employ profitably the most improved methods.

With the cheapening of products and the increased consumption which followed the use of these successive improvements, and the consequent social advance of the community, a revolution in the methods of distribution and international communication became necessary. Inventions multiplied, which so enlarged the industrial world as to render corporations necessary in order to obtain the best economic results. Modern trusts are but a single step farther in the same direction. They are simply the organization of corporations, in the same way that corporations were the organization of individual capitalists.

Trusts, instead of being sudden monopolistic creations that have been sprung on the community by a few designing conspirators, are but the last link in an industrial chain more than a century long; they are no more revolutionary than any one of the previous links, and less so than some of the earlier ones. Each one of these links in the great chain of industrial evolution came and stayed only because it was more profitable than its predecessors to those who employed it; lessened the cost of production and served the community more cheaply. Had it not done this, it could not have sustained itself in competition with the old methods.

That the concentration of capital is necessary to the employment of the best methods in modern industry is too obvious to need discussion. Those who controvert this position may be passed by as unqualified scientifically to discuss the subject. Every labor-saving and price-reducing improvement now in use has involved concentration of capital in some form; in fact, the history of the economic progress of the present century is the history of the concentration of productive capital. To decentralize capital is to barbarize society. The general proposition of the economic necessity of the centralization of capital, therefore, may be regarded as self-evident.

Like all other institutions in society, trusts must be judged by their service to the community. Do they serve the public cheaper and better than did smaller organizations? If they do not, the community has no use for them. In considering this question, however, we must distinguish the spurious from the genuine, and not make economic trusts responsible for the doings of merely uneconomic speculative combinations. One of the chief objections urged against trusts is that they are monopolies. Now, we must beware of attaching too much importance to this charge. The cry "Monopoly" is very likely to be raised against the successful by those who fail. With this calling of names the community has no concern; it is interested only in the economic result. This will depend mainly upon the manner in which the so-called monopoly is acquired. If it is acquired through special legislation, by which competitors can be excluded and prices arbitrarily controlled, it will be monopoly in the objectionable sense. On the other hand, if the control of the market is obtained by furnishing better and cheaper goods, it is clearly an advantage to the consuming public. Now, the great successful trusts have not relied upon special legislation ; on the contrary, they frequently have been obliged to spend large sums of money to prevent themselves from being handicapped by discriminating legislation. Indeed, it is true that, encouraged by the prevalent antagonism to large capitalists, mushroom statesmen have made it a too common practice to concoct threatening legislative measures, which they never expect to have passed, for the purpose of exacting tribute from railroad and other corporations. Of this practice the Union Pacific and the Broadway railroad are conspicuous victims.

Trusts have obtained their industrial supremacy either by improving the quality or lowering the price of the commodities they furnish. Of course, one result of the success of the larger organizations is that smaller and inferior competitors are either absorbed by them or driven from the field. But to this no valid objection can be urged. Those who best serve the community are entitled to the community's support ; otherwise there could be no lowering of prices, and we should still be handicapped by the high cost and poor service of the hand-loom and stage-coach methods such as Russia now enjoys. Therefore, to complain because those who produce most cheaply obtain supremacy is to complain of the advance of civilization.

That the great trusts have obtained their supremacy through their economic superiority is completely demonstrated in the history of the Standard Oil Company, the Western Union Telegraph Company, and our great railway systems. The price of petroleum, for instance, has not only been greatly reduced since the trust was organized, but the quality of the oil has been immensely improved. When petroleum was produced by small companies, and cost four times its present price, its quality was such as to render its use highly dangerous. The daily papers always reported, among the casualties, a number of accidents from lamp explosions. At an immense expense the trust has almost entirely eliminated the explosive element, and at the same time has improved the illuminating quality of the oil and reduced the price about thirty per cent. Moreover, by the introduction of new processes this trust has developed methods for manufacturing several new products from what has hitherto been refuse, with only a fuel value. From this waste is now manufactured naphtha, lubricating oil, paraffine wax, etc., and the price to the public in each case has been greatly lowered. For example, the price of paraffine oil has been reduced from 22 cents to about 11 cents a gallon, and has been improved over 50 per cent. in its lubricating qualities. In 1875 the standard for American paraffine oil by the commercial test, viscosity, was 100 seconds at the temperature of 70; it now tests 150, and its flash point, which in 1875 was 300, is now 380.

In 1875 paraffine oil could not be used for lubricating machinery without the admixture of from 20 to 50 per cent. of animal oil; it can now be used without any animal oil. This is true of several lubricants made from petroleum, especially cylinder oil, which, even for railroad purposes, has superseded tallow and other animal lubricants. Again, in 1875 the price of petroleum cylinder oil was $1.25 a gallon; it is now less than 40 cents. The price of black lubricating oil used for railroad axles was from 15 to 18 cents a gallon in 1875 ; it is now sold at from 7 to 9 cents. The production of paraffine wax since 1870 has been increased from 6,000 to over 20,000 tons a year, and the price has been reduced from 9 to 5 cents a pound. The manufacture of these by-products has involved the use of large quantities of sulphuric acid, which the trust decided to manufacture for its own use, and, through improved processes, has reduced its price from $1\frac{1}{4}$ cents a pound to 8 cents a hundred pounds. It has thus not only greatly reduced the price of its main product but it has converted mere waste into numerous by-products, every one of which has been greatly improved in quality and lowered in price. The cost of cotton-seed oil, sugar, and the transportation and telegraph service, under the control of the most conspicuous trusts and combinations, has fallen in a similar ratio.

There has indeed been a general cheapening of commodities during the last fifty years, but facts everywhere show that the fall in prices has been greatest in those industries where capital is most concentrated; for instance, articles produced by hand-labor are not cheaper, but in most cases dearer, than they were half a century ago,—witness art-engraving, sculpture, wood and stone carving, brick-laying, mason-work, etc. ; and, with the exception of wheat and a few other articles, the price of farm, garden, and dairy products is higher now than in the first quarter of the century. It is in manufactured products that the great reduction in price has taken place. This is because in manufacturing industries only have large capitals and labor-saving machinery been employed. The reason the price of hand-labor products has increased is that wages

have risen with the general rise of civilization, and
none of the labor has been saved by the use of machinery. In agricultural industries machinery has been
introduced only to a limited extent, and hence has not
lessened the cost of production perceptibly more than
the rise of wages has increased it; and agricultural
prices have remained practically static. In manufacturing, through the extensive use of capital, the cost
of production has been reduced by improved machinery
very much more than it has been increased by the rise
in wages, hence the marked lowering of prices. This
distinction is equally marked in different lines of manufacture, the economy in production and the fall of
prices being greatest where the largest capitals and
best methods are employed. Nothing better measures
the real cheapening of products than the purchasing
power of daily wages. We have elsewhere[1] furnished
statistics of wages and prices which show that from 1860
to 1885 the purchasing power, in two hundred staple
articles, of the average weekly wages in twenty mechan-
ical industries increased a little over fifty per cent.
Applying the same test to the production of cotton-seed
oil, petroleum, and sugar, and to railroad and telegraph
service, which are in the hands of the largest combinations, we find that from 1860 to 1890 the average purchasing power of the same wages was increased 236 per
cent., or more than four times as much as those of the
non-trust corporations, as shown in the following table.
Judged by the standard of efficiency of service and
cheapness of product, as here shown, trusts are manifestly a superior form of industrial organization:

[1] Principles of Social Economics, p. 408.

Purchasing power of weekly wages in	1860	1890	Percentage of increase
Cotton-seed oil	18.02 gals.	29.93 gals.	66
Sugar refined.........	90.09 lbs.	152.00 lbs.	67
Freight, New York to Chicago :			
First class........	530.00 "	1317.00 "	148
Second class.......	654.00 "	1520.00 "	132
Third class	822.00 "	1976.00 "	176
Fourth class........	1309.00 "	2822.00 "	115
Telegraph messages ..	8.25 "	31.66 "	283
Petroleum, refined ...	107.89 "	1086.89 "	907

Average percentage of increase......................236

Of course, all trusts have not made so good a showing as these, which we have cited because they are
among the oldest and largest concerns of their kind,
and are, moreover, legitimate economic organizations.
Their success demonstrates the correctness of the principle of capitalistic concentration, and shows that properly conducted trusts are truly beneficial to society.
There are economic and uneconomic trusts, just as
there are the genuine and the spurious in every walk of
life. Economic trusts are those which, like the Standard Oil Company, the Western Union Telegraph Company, the American Sugar Refining Company, and
the great railroad systems, have used their consolidated
capital to acquire profits through economies in production, and have shared the gain with the community
by giving lower prices and better service. All such
contribute to the permanent improvement of society.

There are combinations, however, that have assumed the name without the virtue, and have used
their organization to benefit their promoters at the expense of the public. Although it is true that this stand-
and-deliver method cannot succeed permanently, it can

and does inflict injury for a time. Such is the history of " corners." Several so-called trusts have endeavored to employ this method, conspicuously the copper trust, which, instead of trying to increase its profits by improving the methods of producing copper, has tried to lock up the copper of all the world, and then to exact exorbitant prices or to deprive the community of the use of the metal. But, like Keene with his wheat corner, and the Panama conspiracy it overreached its mark and collapsed, bringing ruin in its fall to many of its projectors. Several other combinations have tried to do substantially the same thing on a smaller scale.

It is this uneconomic use of large capitals, this attempt of a few industrial pirates to exact large profits from the community by raising prices, that has brought trusts into general disrepute. Of course, it would be absurd to condemn legitimate industrial organizations for the misconduct of uneconomic combinations; nevertheless, it should be remembered that public opinion is not discriminating; it is likely to judge a class by its known specimens, and is much more likely to remember those who injure than those who benefit. The prevalent feeling against capitalists in general is encouraged by the direct abuse of successful business men by political editors, reflected and intensified in the fairyland socialism portrayed by all grades of fiction writers from Bellamy to Howells. Strictly speaking, therefore, although much of the opposition to trusts in particular and to capital in general is irrational, it has really been created by the uneconomic conduct of capitalists themselves. The chief reason for this is that capitalists, like laborers, are ignorant

of the subject of industrial economics. For the same
reason that they mistakenly believe in cheap-labor production, they delude themselves with the idea that
they can establish a profitable business by imposing
upon the community; consequently they have succeeded in arousing the hostility of both laborers and
the general public. A little more in this direction, and
they will be handicapped by a network of socialistic,
restrictive legislation. The political atmosphere is
already surcharged with threatening rumors. The
Sherman anti-trust law and the various laws against
trusts, under which the Standard Oil trust has been
forced to disband, foreshadow what is likely to come.
Schemes for graduated taxation of incomes, to con-
fiscate large fortunes and make millionaires impossible,
are being seriously considered by politicians, who, be
it remembered, always stand ready to do whatever
the people, wisely or unwisely, desire to have done.
This would be a serious blow to industrial progress,
and it would be a blow from which large capitalists
would suffer most.   .

The true remedy for the existing hostility to trusts
and large organizations is in the hands of capitalists
themselves. If they would disarm popular opposition,
they must avoid furnishing superficial revolutionists
with an excuse for creating public opinion against
them by refusing all aid, either of money or influence,
to uneconomic enterprises. If our great capitalists
would resolutely take this high economic position, the
smaller ones would be compelled to do likewise, and
the present universal distrust of capitalistic movement
would soon be superseded by universal confidence. It
is to be hoped that the piano and typewriter trusts

now forming and other projected combinations will act
upon this principle, and thus help to create public confidence in the progress of our present industrial system, instead of furnishing additional arguments for its
destruction.

The error of trusts, then, is not the extent of their
concentration of capital or their industrial supremacy;
it is their failure to recognize the economic law of
their existence, namely, *that an increased concentration
of capital and commercial power in fewer hands is justifiable only on the condition of improved service to the
community, either in better quality or lower price of
what is furnished.* Profits are the legitimate reward
of capitalistic enterprise, but they must be obtained by
exploiting nature through improved methods, not by
exploiting the community through higher prices. If
capitalists imagine that any amount of accumulated
wealth can enable them to defy this essential condition,
they are wofully mistaken, and sooner or later they
will have to pay the penalty, either by arrest of their
progress or by entire dispossession of their present
industrial opportunities.

III.

INTEGRITY OF ECONOMIC LITERATURE *

PUBLIC opinion, like public taste, appears periodically to run mad on special topics. The subject upon which popular madness is most pronounced at present is accumulated capital. The chief characteristic of the last half century's industrial development has been the concentration of productive processes, the aggregation of large capital, and consequently the appearance of millionaire capitalists.

Notwithstanding that these large fortunes are chiefly invested in productive enterprises, earning profit only when they are working for the public by cheapening wealth, the fact that the large concerns succeed, while small ones decline, has given rise to the tacit assumption that large capital necessarily implies business dishonesty and public disadvantage for private gain. There is a certain naturalness in this feeling, since those who fail are ever prone to ascribe their failures to somebody else rather than to themselves. It was this feeling that inspired the hand-loom weavers in the beginning of the century to organize mobs to smash the power-looms. The small manufacturers assumed the same injured attitude towards corporations. Small farmers have the same dislike of large farmers. And under the same notion, trade unionists have ever opposed new inventions.

* Published in the *Social Economist* of July 1895.

This feeling has been made a basis of a general doctrine that profits are robbery, and hence that large capitalists are social robbers. The advocates of socialism, populism, single-tax nationalism, and free trade have all tried to make headway by appealing to and inflaming this sentiment. Iconoclastic propagandas on these lines have been so successful that to attack millionaire capitalists is now something of a fad. Under the influence of this prejudice against capital, demagogical misrepresentation is easily palmed off for honest statement and interest in public welfare, undermining the integrity of economic literature.

The latest and worst specimen of this class of literature is "Wealth Against Commonwealth," by Mr. Henry D. Lloyd of Chicago. This is a book of over five hundred pages, purporting to expose the dishonest means by which large corporations have crushed honest business men and defrauded the public. The real aim of the book, however, is to traduce the Standard Oil Company. Mr. Lloyd makes great show of getting his facts from official reports of legislative investigations and court proceedings, to which he makes frequent reference in foot-notes. This gives the book a seeming authority, and the writer's frequent outbursts of patriotic sentiment lend to it a color of sincerity and public interest. This apparent genuineness is further enhanced by a very liberal use of quotation marks, together with the fact that the book bears the imprint of such a reputable house as Harper Bros. On the assumption that a respectable publisher and average literary integrity are proof against deliberate misrepresentation, several high-minded journals have hailed it as an important contribution to economic literature.

As an instance of this, *The Outlook*, edited by the Rev. Dr. Lyman Abbott, who is preëminently zealous in the work of moral reform though somewhat ragged on economics, introduces " Wealth Against Common- wealth " to its readers with the statement that it "is the most powerful book on economics that has appeared in this country since Henry George's ' Progress and Poverty.' . . . . The real greatness of Mr. Lloyd's work lies in its clear massing of evidence unearthed from the records of courts and official investigations, proving to the most sceptical the enormity and persist- ency of the criminal operations by which the wealth of the Standard Oil Company has been amassed. It is the plain, straightforward recital of these facts which brings conviction and arouses indignation."

After a column of this kind of preface, Dr. Abbott says: " To indicate its character, it is better for us to summarize a chapter than to summarize the book. In reading, for example, the story of George Rice, we are more impressed with the meaning of rebates than when we are told the Pennsylvania Railroad paid in this way more than a million a year into the treasury of the Standard Oil Company ; " and then he prints the greater part of one of Mr. Lloyd's three chapters devoted to Mr. Rice's experience in refining oil at Marietta, Ohio, and, as might be expected, concludes by declaring : " The remedy for the evils plainly lies, not in the public control of oil refineries, but in the public control of the public highways."

Dr. Abbott is perfectly right in regarding this blood-curdling chapter as typical of the whole book. It is indeed typical in its inflammatory style ; its violent misrepresentation through garbled statements in quotation marks; and the utter suppression of evidence on the other side.   We have taken the pains to go through the public documents referred to in this book, and it may be said that there is scarcely an honest quotation in it.   Indeed, there seems to be as much downright dishonesty in the quotations from public documents and display of foot-notes as there is demagogy in the high-wrought and indignant perorations.   The dishonesty does not consist in misquotations but in partial and unfair quotations and in always quoting from the testimony of those against the Standard Oil Company to the utter suppression of all rebuttal.

It is just about as fair and honest as it would be for an author to write a book on the American tariff and take all his evidence from the speeches of the democrats in the last (53d) congress.   He would get plenty of testimony against the tariff, but it would be made up, for the most part, of reckless and unscrupulous statements—partly true and largely false, and always unreliable—inspired chiefly by party hatred, political ambition and personal interest.   This is exactly the character of much of the evidence given before political investigating committees.   The greater part of the testimony against the Standard Oil Company is given by persons who failed through being unable to compete with the Standard and were, in fact, in the position of complainants.

While the testimony from both sides was taken by the commission, Mr. Lloyd quotes from the testimony of the complainant and never from that of the defendant, as if the statements of complainants were always the verified and undisputed truth in the case.   Wherever in cases of litigation the decision of the court was in favor of the Standard, he assumes without any evidence whatever that the verdict was due to a corrupt court purchased by the Standard Oil Company. There is throughout the book great vigor of statement, apparent earnestness of purpose, and an intense, lurid high-wrought style with an utter absence of the spirit of fairness and of literary and economic integrity. Between the lines and on the lines, the book bears all the marks of the special pleader who is more intent on winning his case than on telling the truth or promoting a public reform. A few instances will suffice to show the character of the book.

After devoting less than forty pages to other trusts, to give a pretense of general discussion of the subject, he begins his attack upon the Standard Oil Company by describing the character and organization of the "South Improvement Company." He says (p. 46):

"By this contract the railroads had agreed with this company of citizens as follows :

1. To double freight rates.
2. Not to charge them the increase.
3. To give them the increase collected from all competitors.
4. To make any other changes of rates necessary to guarantee their success in business.
5. To destroy their competitors by high freight rates.
6. To spy out the details of their competitors' business.

The increase in rates in some cases was to be more than double. These higher rates were to be ostensibly charged to all shippers, including the thirteen members of the South Improvement Company ; but that fraternity only did not have to pay them yearly. All, or nearly all, the increase it paid was to be paid back again —a "rebate." The increase paid by everyone else—" on all transported by other parties "—was not paid back. It was to be kept, but not by the railroads. These were to hand that, too, over to the South Improvement Company.

This secret arrangement made the actual rate of the South Improvement Company much lower, sometimes half, sometimes less than half, what all others paid. The railroad officials were not to collect these enhanced freight rates from the unsuspecting subjects of his "contract" to turn them into the treasury of the railroads. They were to give them over to the gentlemen who called themselves "South Improvement Company." The "principle" was that the railroad was not to get the benefit of the additional charge it made to the people. No matter how high the railroads put the rates to the community, not the railroad but the improvement company was to get the gain. The railroads bound themselves to charge everyone else the highest nominal rates mentioned. "They shall not be less," was the stipulation. They might be more up to any point; but less they must not be.

The rate for carrying petroleum to Cleveland to be refined was to be advanced, for instance, to 80 cents a barrel. When paid by the South Improvement Company, 40 cents of the 80 were to be refunded to it; when paid by anyone else, the 40 cents were not merely not to be refunded, but to be paid over to his competitor, this aspiring self-improvement company. The charge on refined oil to Boston was increased to $3.07; and, in the same way, the South Improvement Company was to get back a rebate of $1.32 on every barrel it sent to Boston, and on every barrel anyone else sent. The South Improvement Company was to receive sums ranging from 40 cents to $1.32, and averaging a dollar a barrel on all shipments, whether made by itself or others. This would give the company an income of a dollar a day on every one of the 18,000 barrels then being produced daily, whether its members drilled for it, or piped it, or stored it, or refined it, or not."

Now, when Mr. Lloyd wrote this, and there is a whole chapter of twenty-two pages devoted to it, besides repeated references throughout the whole book, he knew that this so-called South Improvement Company was a myth—that it never had any real existence. He knew that it never produced, refined, bought, sold or transported a gallon of oil, nor did a dollar's worth of business of any kind whatever. In short he knew

4

that it was nothing more nor less than a projected scheme which was never born. Consequently, all this effort to create the impression that it compelled railroads to double freight charges on all the competitors of the South Improvement Company, and pay to it the booty, which amounted to a tax on its competitors of $18,000 a day for the permission to do business, is equal to outright misrepresentation.

It would be just as true to say that because a number of persons met in a hotel and agreed that they would raise the price of food so high that a million people would die of starvation, they actually caused the death of a million people, when neither the rise of price, the starvation, nor deaths occurred.

It is also assumed that the Standard Oil Company is responsible for all that the Improvement Company is alleged to have contemplated, whereas the evidence shows no connection between them further than that certain members of the Standard Company subscribed for stock in the Improvement Company, as likewise did many of the Standard Company's most bitter opponents, while other prominent members of the Standard Company were among those who procured the death of the South Improvement Company.

Throughout the entire five hundred pages constant reference is made to this South Improvement Company as if it actually had done all this statement says it intended to do. Such is the kind of economic history Mr. Lloyd is trying to make. The scandalous South Improvement Company story has already found its way into serious economic literature in England. In his "Evolution of Modern Capitalism," published in the Contemporary Science Series, Mr. Hobson reproduces this whole story, together with numerous other mis-statements of fact gathered from similar sources, all of which are presented in the most serious manner as if they were verified data.

Were the evil influence of such misrepresentation limited to its original utterance, this might be a small affair ; but when it is reproduced in permanent and otherwise reliable literature it is quoted as authorita-tive matter and thus becomes a means of polluting the stream of economic knowledge at its very source.

His next chapter, entitled : " You Are Not to Refine," is devoted to working up to white heat the case of a ruined widow. It is narrated under such headings as " The Widow's Cruse," " By the Agent's Conscience," " Judgment-Day Law," etc. This is a case, Mr. Lloyd tells us, of "one of the pioneer manufacturers of Cleveland. He was a prominent member of the First Presbyterian Church, was at one time President of the Young Men's Christian Association, and was active in all enterprises of a religious and benevolent character." He began refining petroleum in 1860, and continued in the business until his death in 1874. After his death his wife continued the business. She is reported as saying : " My husband went into debt just before his death for the first time in his life. For the interests of my fatherless children, as well as myself, I thought it my duty to continue the business. I took seventy-five thousand of the hundred thousand of stock and continued from that time, 1874, until November, 1878, making handsome profits," which, Mr. Lloyd says, were " about twenty-five thousand a year."

He then describes a plot on the part of the Standard Oil Company to ruin the widow, in comparison with

which the methods of the Inquisition were mild and
humane. She finally sold her interest in the works
and good-will for $60,000, agreeing not to re-enter the
business in competition, which is the usual custom
when selling business good-will. She was evidently
made to believe soon afterwards that she had sold for
too little, whereupon she wrote a long letter to the
president of the trust charging him with wronging her
and warning him that he would have to account for
this at the Judgment Day. It appears that $60,000
was about three times what it would cost to construct
new and better facilities than her factories furnished.
The upshot of the whole business was that the trust
offered to return her property if she would return the
money, or offered to sell her one, two or three hundred shares of the stock at the price that had been
paid her for it—all of which she declined.

Yet, in the face of the fact that she could have her
property back—which is not usual in business transactions, if there is any profit in keeping it—or that she
could have shares in the stock under the new management, where the business was expected to be more
profitable, or actually receive for her property three
times what it would cost to replace it, Mr. Lloyd
devotes a whole chapter to a most heartrending
description of how this widow was robbed and wronged.
In order to give a semblance of basis for his case, he
says: " The cost of the work is not the standard of
value in such transactions." He assumes that because at one time this woman's property yielded a
profit of $25,000 a year, its value should still have
been estimated on an earning capacity of that amount.
But why, then, did she refuse to take it back? The

fact is that the property had passed its large profit-making stage, and was rapidly being superseded by improved methods which would soon reduce its value to that of old iron, which is commonly the case with factories of all kinds. She evidently knew this and preferred the money to the factory.

From all the facts given in this nameless widow's case, it is clearly making " much ado about nothing." The whole chapter is a frantic attempt to play upon sentiment by weaving a malicious and virtually lying threat through the whole statement, with the obvious purpose of creating a false impression. There is nothing in the case to show that the woman was wronged, except the vicious inferences of the writer. On the contrary many of the facts tend to show that she was generously treated; that what she obtained for her plant was largely gain, since, if she had not sold it, it would soon have become valueless through the superior methods employed by the new competing concerns.

Another instance of martyrdom to which Mr. Lloyd devotes a sixteen-page chapter with the suggestive title : " I Want to Make Oil " is the case of Mr. Van Syckel, an inventor. This story is a duplicate of hundreds and perhaps thousands of cases of inventors—except that few are told with such harassing and wrath-inspiring force as is this one. It is a general characteristic of inventors that they are greatly lacking in executive ability or practical sense. While they originate the abstract idea, they very seldom complete the process. Before an invention can become usable, it generally has to be very much improved ; indeed, it has practically to be evolved by an indefinite number of experiments and, not infrequently, after years of trial and an expenditure of thousands upon thousands of dollars, it just fails.

It would probably be a moderate estimate to say that hundreds, perhaps thousands, of such inventions fail for every one that is reduced to practical use. In every instance the inventor, even though he is paid a salary for several years, while developing his invention, believes that he is swindled out of a fortune-making discovery; whereas, it is more frequently true that thousands of dollars have been wasted to give him an opportunity to develop a failure. Of course, this is the only way that inventions can be developed, but the fact remains that not one per cent. of inventions are a success.

A statement recently appeared in the public print to the effect that the Western Union Telegraph Company made a business of "gobbling up," through purchase, of course, all inventions in telegraphy, and that they then stowed them away or destroyed them for the purpose of preventing the inventors from realizing a fortune out of their discoveries and heading off successful competitors. One would think the obvious absurdity of such a statement would prevent its passing the blue pencil of any sane editor. Nothing but insanity could prompt such action. The Western Union could have no motive for suppressing or destroying an invention that had any economic merit. Indeed, it spends thousands of dollars every year to discover new devices which shall enable it to reduce the cost of doing its business, as do all large corporations and not a few individual concerns.

Now, Mr. Lloyd's story of Mr. Van Syckel is precisely of this kind. It recites what doubtless Mr. Van

Syckel believed, *viz.* : that he discovered a continuous process of distilling oil—an improvement that would be a saving of from thirty to thirty-five per cent. of labor and cost in the process of distilling. According to Mr. Lloyd's story, the new process was demonstrated to be a complete success, and yet the Standard Oil Company, after having paid Van Syckel "$125 a month while he was testing and improving the invention and $75 a month afterwards, deliberately suppressed the invention; would neither use it nor permit anybody else to use it, nor pay Van Syckel for it." This is conduct which nobody but malicious idiots could be guilty of, and only an infatuated fanatic could expect intelligent people to believe such a tale.

If that invention had been a success, nothing would induce the Standard Oil Company to refrain from using it. Whatever else may be said of the members of the Standard Oil Company, they were never suspected of throwing away the possibility of increased profits for a sentiment. They may have been heartless, but they never before were charged with being idiots. Nothing can be more conclusive proof of the fallacy of this story than the fact that no such process is in use anywhere in the world. The Standard Oil Company would doubtless give half a million dollars to-morrow for such an invention, and yet, in order to make out that the Standard Oil Company exists chiefly for evil, Mr. Lloyd asks the public to believe that, solely to injure a poor old inventor, it is suppressing a discovery by which it could make millions. And the most surprising part of it all is that such a respectable house as Harper Bros. could be induced to publish such stuff as sane literature, and such men as the Rev. Lyman

Abbott can swallow it all without a question as if it were rational and verified truth.

We now come to the "Rice" or "Marietta" case, which operated so effectually upon the heart-strings of the editor of *The Outlook.* Mr. Lloyd has laid himself out to make the reader's blood boil with indignation in this instance. He has given three whole chapters to it which bristle throughout with insinuating quotation marks, so used as to misrepresent by what they omit. In Mr. Lloyd's hands the "Rice" case is really a fine piece of revolution-creating literature. It is well calculated to incite the mob to a rich-killing or mansion-sacking crusade.

After describing Mr. Rice as coming from the "Green Mountains of Vermont" and entering "the oil business when he and it were young," and building up "a new industry and a new place," he devotes eight pages to showing how the plot to ruin him was worked, and says (page 206):

"The railroad over which he ran his tank-car doubled his freight to 35 cents a barrel, from 17½. That was not all. The same railroad brought oil to the combination's Marietta refineries at 10 cents a barrel, while they charged him 35. That was not all. The railroad paid over to the combination 25 cents out of every 35 cents he paid for freight. If he had done all the oil business at Marietta, and his rival had put out all its fires and let its works stand empty, it would still have made 25 cents a barrel on the whole output."

No one could read this without being inspired by the feeling it is intended to convey, *viz. :* that it was a high-handed outrage which would justify summary treatment, and when one learns from a most passionate portrayal, much of which is repeated several times in different forms, that by this means an honest, enterprising man, whose success his daughters helped to secure by working in the business with him, was finally ruined and his family wrecked, it is difficult to suppress the impulse to inaugurate lynch law, but if we read the report of testimony taken by the Fiftieth Congress, in which the whole case is printed, we find that much more inflammation is imparted to it by Mr. Lloyd than by the facts.   Briefly stated, the facts are these [1]:

Mr. Rice was an oil refiner in Marietta, the market for which was Cleveland, Ohio.   The oil was partly taken through pipe lines and partly by rail.   The railroad agreed to charge for the entire distance, including pipe lines, 35 cents a barrel for shipment, 25 cents of which was to be paid to the owners of the pipe line for its portion of the service; the railroad to have 10 for its. Consequently, all oil shipped from Marietta to Cleveland was charged 35 cents a barrel, subject to the above divisions between the owners of the pipe line and the owners of the railroads.   This applied to all shippers, one of whom was Mr. Rice.   Now, the Standard Oil Company owned the pipe line, hence it paid only the 10 cents which belonged to the railroad for its portion of the service.   There had been considerable friction between Mr. Rice and the Standard Oil Company, and he had laid a pipe line of his own, and therefore did not ship through the pipes of the Standard.   This arrangement for 35 cents a barrel was originally made for all oil that came from Marietta, regardless of whether it used

---

[1] Testimony taken by the House of Representatives, 1888; pp. 274–5.

the Standard pipe line or not, so that Mr. Rice was charged the 35 cents a barrel although he sent it to the railroad through his own pipe line. That is to say, he was charged 35 cents, though he used the railroad service only; the 25 cents for pipe line service went to the Standard just the same as if his oil had gone through their line.

This was an obvious hardship. Still, it was of the same character as many other transportation arrangements, such as the long and short haul principle whereby shippers for the shorter distance pay more for the same amount of freight than shippers for a longer distance, and there are conditions under which this is distinctly economic and justifiable. All the elevated, cable cars and electric railroads in New York and other large cities are run on the same principle. They charge as much to ride a block as to ride five miles. This seems to be something of an American idea. In London, for instance, the underground railroads and the busses everywhere have different rates for different distances.

We do not cite this, however, to justify the treatment of Mr. Rice, but only to show that it was not an entirely new and novel method of making transportation charges. If this arrangement had been made permanent and had resulted in Mr. Rice's ruin it would go far to justify Mr. Lloyd's position, regardless of the fact that it was a practise commonly adopted in railroading. But the truth is that the arrangement was a temporary affair lasting only a very short time. It was made by an agent of the pipe line company, and when brought to the attention of the company's counsel it was, under his advice, discontinued, and, what is of still more importance, the whole amount of this charge for pipe line service which Mr. Rice did not receive was less than $250 *and every penny of it was returned to him*, so that Mr. Rice finally lost nothing by this so-called over-charge.

These facts are nowhere mentioned by Mr. Lloyd, although he spreads the discussion of the case over three whole chapters. Everything he says regarding the matter is intended to convey the idea that Mr. Rice paid 35 cents a barrel while the Standard Oil Company only paid 10 cents and the extra 25 cents went into the pockets of the Standard Oil Company, and that this continued until Mr. Rice was ruined by the process.

Such a statement of the case is equivalent to positive misrepresentation, especially when accompanied by pages upon pages of inflammatory insinuations, charging it all to the mythical South Improvement Company.

We have no idea that the members of the Standard Oil Company, individually or collectively, are very much better or worse than other people. Their methods have been the methods of business men generally. Self-interest and not the golden rule has doubtless been their chief inspirer. Nor have we any desire to hold them up as models except to the extent that they have introduced improvements into productive processes and business methods. Nor are we in the least opposed to the full exposure of any economic mistakes they have made or social wrongs they may have committed. It is only by the exposure of the wrong that the right can be permanently established. But what we are particularly interested in is the integrity of economic literature.

We protest against the wholesale misrepresentations of industrial facts and the poisoning of economic motives merely to gratify the ravings of fanatical opposition to aggregated capital; and we specially protest against such wholesale libels passing for reliable economic information. It is more important to maintain the integrity of economic literature than to overthrow the largest trust that ever existed.

Such books as "Wealth Against Commonwealth" are calculated to do more to invalidate history and corrupt the morals of public thought and action than could a hundred trusts. If the channels of information are to be polluted with impunity by wholesale misrepresentation of industrial data, then the integrity of our economic information, the validity of our industrial history and social literature, are destroyed.

IV.

ARE LUXURIES WASTED WEALTH?*

THE public mind at the present time is in something
of a fever of opposition to wealth. The great object
seems to be to find some way of suppressing wealth or
punishing those who have any. If the rich devote their
wealth to productive enterprise, we call for legislation
to suppress them lest they should make any profits.
We are having a flood of legislation against trusts, and a
trust is anything that is large and successful and makes
any profits, or introduces any improvements into the
business. A bill is pending in Massachusetts, for instance, imposing a penalty of from $100 to $5,000 fine,
or imprisonment for a year, or both, upon any person
who, going into business, lessens competition and drives
others out, and the parties driven out also have right
of damages against their successful competitors. On
the other hand, if the rich spend their money socially,
we raise a great cry throughout the country about
their criminal extravagance, and the ministers and
sentimentalists are all up in arms. If, finally, they go
abroad and take their millions with them, we assail
them as being mean and unpatriotic, while if they
simply hoard up their wealth and do nothing with it

---

* Lecture delivered in New York City, Feb. 3, 1897.

we denounce them as misers. It would seem that the only thing for a rich man to do is to get rid of his wealth as soon as possible and reduce himself to the same state of poverty that the poor enjoy and find so satisfactory and desirable. Then, and then only, it seems, will they be able to stand high in the public favor.

The Bradley Martin ball is one of the prominent incidents that is calling forth a good deal of discussion on this subject of wealth. Is this affair to be regarded as a social calamity, and ought public sentiment and legislation to be invoked to put a stop to it, or is there another side to it, and are we entitled to pass judgment upon a whole series of public and social institutions because there are a few butterflies here and there who do not know how to exercise good taste in their expenditures, and exhibit an abnormal desire for mere vain display?

Very much of this sort of opposition looks like turning back to the conditions against which the world has been struggling for centuries. For instance, the New York *Press* this morning made a great uproar because a man in overalls was not allowed to go into the Metropolitan Museum. Of course he was not, nor should he have been. To make that sort of thing respectable throughout the community would be the worst possible thing that could be done for the workingman. Laborers when they visit places of that nature ought to observe the same decencies and civilized customs that are observed by the rest of the public, for they will then insist upon wages sufficient to enable them to meet those requirements. Let it be established that overalls are good enough to go to museums in, and

they will soon be good enough to go to church in, and
to the opera in, and everywhere in, and we shall have
really very little need of decent clothes at all, and our
wages and civilization, following along that same line
of ideas, will eventually get down to the overalls level.
We do not want to turn back to any one-suit-of-clothes
state of civilization. It has taken centuries for the
workingman to assert and establish a standard of living
that shall demand something better than that, and the
superficial clamorers who are insisting upon the social
recognition of overalls as good enough for all places
and occasions are really the worst enemies the workingmen have. What we want is that laborers shall insist
upon clothing fit for such places, and insist upon wages
sufficient to buy such clothing. We do not want five-
cent dinners, and bean-pod soup at two cents, and overalls on Sunday, and we will not have them.

As early as the fourteenth century the struggle over
this question began. The workingmen in England
made their first efforts for an increase of wages, and
they were at once legislated against. They were not
to ask for more pay, and it was prescribed very carefully what they were to eat and wear and have in their
houses. They should not wear clothes that cost more
than eight pence a yard, and should have practically
no meat, and should piece out, from time to time, with
the "offal from the master's table," and so on. And
later on, when people began to have windows and
chimneys in their houses, the laborers were denounced
as inexcusably extravagant and as enemies of the progress of the realm, because they too began to want
windows, and doors on hinges, and objected to having
the smoke go out through the door instead of up a

chimney. Of course the laborers finally won their
struggle, and little by little gained the privilege of eat-
ing and dressing and living as they chose. Things
seem to have undergone a remarkable turn-about since
then. Now it is the laborers themselves who are dic-
tating what shall be eaten and worn by the rich, and
how they shall conduct themselves. Having struggled
for centuries against just this sort of interference with
personal liberty, they are now endeavoring to apply it
in turn to the very classes whom they were once de-
nouncing for trying to inflict it upon them. They
were right, of course, in insisting upon windows and
chimneys and such food and clothing as they liked and
could get, on the ground of personal liberty, but personal liberty to-day, it appears, has no application to
fancy balls.

After about four centuries of this struggle on the
part of the wage-workers, came Adam Smith with his
gospel that the secret of social progress is parsimony ;—
use as little and save as much as possible. He thought
it was prodigality for a workingman to burn a candle
after eight o'clock at night, and on the other hand that
a rich man was a very bad thing to have in any town.
That idea of parsimony has permeated English economic thought down almost to the present day, and workmen have taken it on, to the extent of holding the
idiotic doctrine that everybody who consumes more
than they do is inflicting an injury upon society.

About a week ago the New York *Journal* interviewed the secretary of the United Garment Workers'
Union, and Prof. Felix Adler, on the subject of this ball.
The labor leader said that luxuries meant wealth
wasted, and Prof. Adler said that the laboring men

would not get any real benefit from the ball. As you know, I regard almost everything affecting the welfare of the community as turning upon the way it affects the laborers. If balls were bad things for the laborers I should be opposed to them; if they are good for them, I favor the balls.

There was a time, as I have said, when the laborers did not have chimneys or windows in their houses, no furniture, practically no decent clothing, and lived upon bread and herring and barley beer, and got sixpence a day wages. Now, how have the things come into existence that furnish the appointments of the homes occupied by the average citizen of to-day in the more advanced countries? Has it been by anything the workingmen have done? Have they introduced any such industries as silk weaving, for instance? Not so. There never would have been silk enough made to go into one dress of a mechanic's wife if silk had not been first used by kings and the aristocracy and those who were willing to pay the great sums necessary in the first instance to have it made. It was then the exceptional social need, and it was called extravagance, just as Adam Smith called burning a candle after eight o'clock extravagance for the workingman. After the very rich begin to have these things and pay the high prices necessary to get them, then the next below begin to contrive so as to get some themselves, and finally there is enough demand to establish a small permanent business, and as a result the price falls a little. Then a still wider circle of consumers come in and begin to use the once unapproachable luxury, and this permits in turn still lower prices, and by the repetition of this process it finally gets down to

5

the level of all of us, and the articles are produced in immense factories by the best and cheapest machine methods, and at the minimum cost. It is in this way that we have come into the enjoyment of practically everything we have outside of the crudest necessities.

Those of you who are familiar with European cities know that when the court is away from London or Berlin business goes into mourning, laborers are out of work, and everything is stagnant. Why? Because when the court goes to London the aristocracy goes there and what is called the London season sets in, and that not only puts in circulation several millions of dollars, but gives employment to thousands and makes all the difference between panic-stricken London and prosperous London, and it is panic-stricken London that tells its story in Whitechapel and the East End. If the garment makers' secretary I have mentioned understood the first principles of the situation he would know that variation of social taste is the very life of his industry. Take China. They have had no change in the cut of their smock for a thousand years. Nobody needs to have a new coat because coats are made to last a lifetime, and very often the same coat will be willed from father to son, and finally worn out by him as a night-shirt. I tell you, any country in which one coat will last a lifetime is a country having neither taste, high social standard, high wages, intelligence, nor freedom.

The opera is in town, and that, too, is called a waste. Will the workingmen and mechanics go? Of course not. They, at least, will waste nothing on it. It has to be supported by the comparatively rich. Now, suppose you suppressed the opera as an extravagance. You would suppress the highest development of music, and help to take out perhaps the most refining, softening and cultivating force in civilization. As a result of the opera we have thousands of musicians preparing for that work and falling a little short, and we get the benefit of them in concerts and churches and in our homes. Music becomes a common accomplishment. The opera is one of the contributions that the rich make to society, not intentionally as such, of course, but the social law is stronger than their desires. I am willing that they should be foolish, perhaps, for a while, because they cannot stop the rest of us from getting the benefit of what they introduce.

I say, therefore, that there is no greater error than to describe luxuries as wasted wealth. There is hardly a single thing that has become the customary necessity of civilization that was not once a luxury—an extravagance converted into a necessity by common social use. Diogenes, you know, when he saw the shepherd boy scooping up water in his hand, said: "What an economy that is; what need have we of cups when nature has already given us hands to drink from!" So it is. Just think of the number of things we could get along without. If we would only get along without cups and what cups imply, we could close up all the factories in the United States and effectually turn back the dial of civilization to the pre-Mosaic type. The fact is, every comfort and convenience we have acquired, over and above what is represented by Diogenes' shepherd boy, has been a luxury, relatively to what was before, and in that development we have simply the record of man's growth out of barbarism into civilization and enlightenment. It is these very luxuries converted into necessities that make the difference between the American laborer's standard of living and that of the Chinaman or African. If these luxuries had been nipped in the bud there would be no difference now between New York and Poland. To-day's luxuries are to-morrow's necessities, if society progresses. It is only in that way that the advantages of civilization can ever be extended to the working people. They are now enjoying, in common use, comforts and refinements that to their fathers would have been unthought-of extravagance. Henry II. slept on a bed of rushes, but we would have a half-dozen revolutions before we would get anywhere near that condition again. The difference between rushes and beds is the result of the conversion, through several centuries, of what were then luxuries into what are now necessities for all.

In 1875 I was called to a factory town in Connecticut where there was a strike in progress. I found in operation there the "truck" system, under which the corporation kept a store with all the supplies it thought its employees should have, and had a record of the wages in one book and purchases in the other, managing generally so that the two about balanced. At that time, many of the employees had not drawn a cent in wages for months, thanks to truck-system bookkeeping. They had a church there, and pew rent was regularly charged up on the books, also. In my interview with the employer he complained a great deal about the growing extravagance of his employees. There had lately been a great strike in Fall River, and his employees were all happy and contented until they heard of that strike. As soon as Fall River people began to come there, and labor agitators began holding meetings, trouble began. The men began spending their money on railroad fare to attend meetings, and the women wanted to go to town every week at least, and bought frivolous things that they never used to want, and the result was that they were striking against a 10 per cent. reduction with which they would have been perfectly contented if they had never heard of cities at all. All their notions and extravagances were so much pure waste, said the manager.

It was not waste at all. Anything that adds a new thought or a new comfort or a new entertainment or refinement to human life is a positive gain, and not a waste. All new things are not good, but in the process of using we eliminate the vicious and keep the good. Newly discovered articles of food sometimes contain poison, but do we on that account abandon them and go back to the coarser diet? Not at all. We call in chemistry to purify the new thing and make it fit for permanent use. If the laboring class could have been kept wearing sheepskins, they would have been earning 10 cents a day now instead of $2 or $3, and we should have had a 10-cent-a-day civilization. There is no greater mistake than for the working class to set themselves against the social innovations at the top of society, because there is not a single thing that is introduced there that does not percolate down. We see an example in the case of the servant girls, who are complained of because they are getting so particular about their privileges and exemptions and so on, and because of their extravagance in dress, and bad taste, and all that. In reality that is the hopeful side. It means the beginning of better conditions and less hard work, more freedom and more civilization, for the servant girl class. Their taste is poor, but do you expect them to wait until they have become artists before they wear bonnets? That is the beginning of their education. If it is true that they put on gloves over dirty hands, all right, they have got the gloves on at least, and that does three things, hides the dirt, starts a glove factory, and starts the person wearing the gloves into the society of others who wear gloves, and they notice that these others have clean hands, and finally begin to wash their own. The truth is, all social refinement begins with more or less of artificial veneering, but finally it penetrates the character and results in genuineness. Cleanliness is not the first sign of civilization that gets into the slums. If you put in bath tubs too early they may be used for coal bins, as has been found from actual experience.

Of course the Bradley Martin ball is not being gotten up as a philanthropic enterprise, and we need not expect it to be. It is surprising, but true, that the bulk of the best things we have were not introduced from the best motives. If we were never to have a railroad until those who built it did so for philanthropic motives, none would ever be built. They are built because we ride and pay fare. We can get railroads simply by making them profitable to the projectors by riding on and using them. Personally, I expect that this ball is a sort of social butterfly affair. The Bradley Martins made a great effort to get a daughter married to a foreign prince, and that meant that they would spend their money abroad. We do

not want that.   What this country needs is that our
wealth should be spent here.   I do not want any person who can afford to live better than I can to come
down to my level.   I want all the rest of you to help
me get up to his level, and the more there are like
him the better my chance of success in that line.   I
do not like to see American capitalists spending their
money abroad, and changing their citizenship because
they cannot get the sort of social life here that they
want.   But, if we are going to assail and punish them
every time they endeavor to introduce new social life
here, we can hardly blame them much for going where
it already exists.   What we ought to do is to encourage the growth of a cultivated class here, who shall
expend their millions in beautifying our own country
with great parks and estates, and in establishing a
social standard that shall act as a constant incentive
to all that is below.   If you can make it impossible
for millionaires to live here, you can succeed in keeping back the growth of American civilization.   You
can make it certain that whatever we have in the
higher forms of social, musical, artistic and literary
life, will be of the second rate order, because we shall
have no class able to pay for the best.   What we want
is to encourage our own wealthy classes to expend
their riches here, so that in satisfying their own desires they shall at the same time, in spite of themselves perhaps, be promoting in the highest and most
efficient sense American art, architecture and science,
and American social life.

V.

LARGE AGGREGATIONS OF CAPITAL*

ARE large aggregations of capital necessary to modern progress? The only point of view from which this question can properly be considered is the welfare of the community. There are two ways in which the productive machinery of society can promote public welfare. One is by improving the quality of wealth produced, and the other by lessening its cost to the public. Whether the instruments of production should be owned by the public as demanded by socialism, or be held in small quantities, as under the domestic methods which prevailed before the Hargreaves, Arkwright, Crompton and Cartwright inventions of the eighteenth century, or by increasingly large corporate concerns, as to-day, turns entirely upon which of these forms of industrial organization will most efficiently furnish the community with consumable wealth, in respect to both quality and price. The owners of capital or productive instruments have absolutely no claim upon the public consideration on any other grounds than efficiency of service to the public, as creators of wealth. Capital should be regarded as a tool, and as a tool only; and the use of any tool is justifiable only so long as it will do its work as well as or better than other tools that are available.

---

*Published in the New York *Independent*, of March 4, 1897, and reprinted in *Gunton's Magazine* of May 1897.

72

The history of concentrated capital is manifestly the history of productive economy and efficiency. Nearly all the great productive economies giving superior quality and reduced prices have been confined to those industries where corporate capital and factory methods have been employed. Take, for instance, cotton, silk, woolen and other fabrics. Common cotton cloth, which as late as 1830 cost seventeen cents a yard, is now quoted at less than four cents ; and so along the whole line. Products of iron, steel and wood have been reduced solely by these processes from 30 to 60 and in some instances 80 per cent., which means that the public have received, in each instance, a superior product for this constantly diminishing price. If we turn to the class of industries in which capital has not been concentrated, or only to a slight extent, we find that the reverse is true, and prices have not lessened with the progress of society.

The great era of machine methods in this country is since 1860. According to the senate report, which was so comprehensive and exhaustive, there were fifty-eight classes of products the prices of which had increased since 1860. Some had risen 100 per cent., and a very large number from 30 to 70 per cent. With one or two exceptions they were all agricultural or raw material products, in which the concentration of capital and the use of machinery had been very slight. On the other hand, the tables give 140 groups of manufactured products in which capital is considerably concentrated and machinery used extensively, and in all prices had fallen from 6 to 40 per cent. The fall in the prices of products produced by capitalistic methods was enough greater than the rise in the prices where hand labor and small capital were used to make an average fall in prices of about 4 per cent., and a rise in wages of 68 per cent. That is to say, through the processes of capitalistic methods, from 1860 to 1891, the purchasing power of a day's work was increased slightly over 72 per cent., which is only another way of saying that concentrated capital increased the public welfare 24 per cent. every ten years since 1860.

Every step in the industrial progress of society has had to encounter a popular opposition. There seems to be an indefinite impression abroad that the corporation has more of the element of conspiracy in it than the individual or firm type ; hence, that the aggregation of capital in the United States is more inimical to public welfare than in other countries. This, however, is psychological rather than economic. Corporations, while not peculiar to the United States, are more prevalent here than elsewhere for definitely good and sufficient economic reasons. In Europe the progress has been sufficiently slow so that native capital could accumulate fast enough to keep up with the demands of industrial growth. In this country the case has been quite different. For reasons it is not necessary to enumerate here our industrial development has been so rapid and colossal that we were wholly unable to create the individual capital necessary to supply the needs of industry. Consequently the corporate means of capitalizing was evolved, so that European wealth as well as the scattered pennies of our own people could be utilized to make possible the great railroad and other undertakings in this country, which have no parallel in any other part of the world. Had we been compelled to wait for the development of individual capital in the non-corporate form, this development would probably have been delayed half a century. Corporations, therefore, are peculiarly American institutions, not because they contain any inferior element, but because they are the utilization of the cooperative spirit made necessary by our exceptionally rapid industrial progress.

It is the universal testimony of history that the aggregation of capital is indispensable to modern progress. There is no phase of industrial progress which has taken place without it. In those countries where the least concentration of capital has occurred, civilization is most backward and progress most sluggish. So, too, of industries. Those industries in the most advanced countries which have participated least in the concentration of capital have made the least progress. Their progress has been less, both in the use of wealth-cheapening methods and in the social effect upon the population. There is no phase of industrial life anywhere, in any country, that does not reveal this characteristic,—witness the southern states.

During the last twenty years, however, a new phase of the corporate form of industrial organization has appeared, viz., the trust. Properly speaking, the trust is simply a larger form of corporation. It is the integration of smaller corporations into one enterprise, in the same way that the corporation was the integration of individuals into one enterprise. It is against this last form that public suspicion is now directed, and legislation in many of the states is being asked for and enacted. It is important in this connection to say that trusts proper, i. e., the concentration of capital into productive corporations, are not to be confounded with mere trade agreements, like the steel combine, the nail combine, the copper combine, wheat corners, etc., whose only effect is to put up or keep up prices. Such combines are not an increased concentration of productive power, but only an increased unanimity among the sellers of products to keep up or put up prices.

Among *bona fide* trusts, which are genuine integrations of capital into larger concerns for productive purposes, the opposite effect has been produced, viz., an improvement in the product and a lowering of the price. In speaking, therefore, of the large accumulations of capital, I wish always to be understood to mean large concentration of capital into one management for productive purposes. Among the conspicuous examples of this kind of aggregation are the Standard Oil trust, the sugar trust, and the cotton-seed oil trust. Of a similar nature are the great railroad and telegraph corporations. . . . . .[1]

Without going into further details, it is manifest that in every line of production where the aggregation of capital has increased, for permanent productive purposes, the effect has been to improve the quality of the commodity or service and reduce the price to the public. But there are many other aspects of the subject in which the public is interested, besides the matter of prices and quality of commodities. Among these are the effect on wages and the permanency of employment.

---

[1] The data which here followed is omitted because it appears in other of the papers in this volume, particularly Nos. I, XVI, and XVII.

With reference to wages the question is quite simple. It is such a well known fact as only barely to need stating, that these large concerns never tend to lower the wages in the industries in which they operate, but on the contrary always pay the highest prevailing wages. In all the industries where great concentration of capital has taken place the wages have increased, except in particular instances where, through the introduction of machinery, a new class of labor has been employed, as substituting women for men and young people for adults, which has been something of a feature throughout the whole factory system. It is by this process that so many new occupations have been opened to women.

The question of permanent employment is scarcely less important than that of wages. Indeed, the uncertainty of employment is one of the most baneful effects of modern industry. The introduction of new machinery and the tendency to overproduce and so glut the market and finally compel temporary suspension has been one of the constant sources of industrial and social perturbation. The tendency of the concentration of productive capital is one of the most effective, if not the only, means of remedying this constant social calamity. In the first place, the larger the investment of capital the greater the loss from any interruption of productive activity. The expenses are so enormous that a short stoppage in many instances would more than neutralize the profits of a whole year. Consequently, the larger the concern the greater the effort accurately to adjust its productive capacity to the market demand for its product, so as to avoid loss from interruption. Industrial depression can never be elimi-

nated until the relation of productive enterprise to
consumption is reduced to some degree of intelligent
precision, which the small go-as-you-please producer
can never do.

The essential economic features of large aggregations of capital, then, are : (1) That by the use of larger
and superior methods they improve the quality and reduce the price of commodities : (2) They are more favorable than smaller concerns to an increase in wages : (3)
By introducing scientific precision into industry, they
tend to increase the permanence of employment and reduce the tendency to industrial depression. Manifestly,
therefore, the tendency to large aggregations of capital in productive enterprise is economically sound,
socially advantageous, and necessary to modern progress.

We now come to the second part of the question
under discussion, viz. : Under what limitations this
capitalistic aggregation should go on.   The limitations
to economic development should always be economic
rather than political or statutory.   Statutory restrictions to the use of capital involve arbitrary and usually
harmful hindrance to the free mobility of economic
forces.   These restrictions are usually the result of an
adverse public sentiment, created by the failure of the
captains of industry to recognize their true economic
relation to the community.   The concentration of capital, like the concentration of all power in society, involves the surrender of a certain amount of productive
individuality in the community.   This can never be
justifiable, nor will it permanently be tolerated, unless
it results in giving to the community a full equivalent
in greater economic advantages.

The economic law of permanent productive integration is that increased concentration of capital and power in fewer hands is economically justifiable and socially tolerable only on the condition of improved services to the community, in better quality or lower prices of what is furnished. Profits are the legitimate reward of capitalistic enterprise; but they should always be obtained by exploiting nature through improved methods, and never by exploiting the community through higher prices. The failure of capitalists to recognize this principle as the inexorable economic law of their existence is sure to bring social antagonism which will result in some form of arbitrary, uneconomic restrictions, detrimental alike to capital and the community. Capitalists who imagine that any amount of accumulated wealth can enable them to defy this social law are greatly mistaken, and sooner or later will have to pay the penalty by the arrest of their progress, if not by the entire dispossession of their present industrial opportunities.

The present anti-trust movement throughout the country is the result of a disregard by capitalists of this economic law of productive integration. The uneconomic combines already referred to, which are a constant violation of this principle, coupled with other political and social disturbances, have tended to create a public sentiment against accumulated capital, *per se.* As is always the case in social revolts, the genuine are arraigned with the spurious and all are put under the ban.

Any legal restrictions, in the sense of limiting the amount of capital used by a single concern, would be a fatal obstruction to economic progress. Instead of

applying arbitrary limitation to the aggregation of
capital, the real reforms to be sought are in the education of the capitalist and the public in regard to the
true relation of capital to the community.

VI

FACTS FROM THE OIL REGIONS *

PROBABLY there is no concern in the world which is the subject of so much suspicion, and psychological as well as industrial antagonism, as the Standard Oil Company. People who know nothing whatever of the oil business, of the industry, history, methods or results of the company, feel perfectly competent to pass judgment, always of course against the trust. This company seems to occupy very much the same position in the industrial sentiment of the community that Satan does in the atmosphere of theology. It is regarded as the evil genius, which is the cause of all the bad and none of the good in the oil industry.

We have had occasion several times to discuss at length the economic effects of the Standard Oil Company on the petroleum industry. Heretofore, however, we have considered the question only on the side of the manufactured article—refined oil—the reason for this being that public discussion has been devoted mostly to that side of the subject. The law-suits, legislative investigations, and practically all anti-trust schemes and literature, have been directed against the " monopoly " in oil refining.

It would be a mistake to assume, however, that

---

* Published in *Gunton's Magazine* of September 1897.

6

the Standard Oil Company has no enemies among the producers. One has only to go into the oil regions and spend a little time among the people in the land of derricks to learn that the crushing hand of the trust is also upon every producer of crude petroleum ; that every man who has a well on his farm, in his back yard, or at his front door, is being robbed day and night and Sundays by the Standard Oil Company.

At first it is difficult to resist the impression that there must be considerable truth in this universal indictment. Such places as Allentown, Bolivar and Richburg, N. Y., show all the symptoms of industrial despair and social decline. Most of the buildings were never touched by a paint brush and there are almost none that ever had the freshening influence of a second coat. Dirt, neglect, broken windows, depleted door-steps, moral inertia, and an utter lack of social life and personal energy, characterize the entire region. It looks as if the hard hand of adversity had visited every household, and all this is attributed to the Standard Oil Company, and generally believed by the public.

The facts connected with the production of crude petroleum, which are little known to the public, represent an extraordinary set of industrial conditions. Through its immense development, the Standard Oil Company has become practically the only purchaser of crude oil. In some of the oil fields, conspicuously those of Allegany county, New York, it has not only become the purchaser of the product but it has finally become the practical surety of every small-well owner, so that they are not undersold or driven out of business by more successful competitors. But for the influence exercised by the Standard Oil Company, fully a quarter and probably a half of the smaller-well owners in the Allegany field would long ago have been forced out of business, and the income from their one, two, three-barrel a day wells been entirely cut off.

The oil producing industry is unique. There is nothing like it in any other line of human effort. With the exception of sinking the well and finding the oil, it affords an almost automatic income without effort, responsibility, or hardly any care. All an oil producer has to do is simply to furnish the well and the Standard Oil Company will do all the rest. The trust owns the pipe lines that convey the oil from the wells to the refineries. When a producer sinks a well and finds oil, all he has to do is to notify the company and it will lay the pipe connecting it with his tank, bear all the expense of transportation, and take all the product whether it needs it or not. The well owner simply has a tank into which he pumps his oil, and as fast as he pumps it he can let it into the trust pipes and draw his money. The trust sustains about the same relation to the well owner that the government would to the silver-mine owner under the free coinage of silver, namely, takes all the product, regardless of how much it is or whether it is needed, and pays "spot cash" for it. There is no other industry in the world where the producers have such absolutely unlimited market, such ease of sale and such complete guarantee against loss. No agents or drummers are needed ; not even skill in bargaining is necessary. The most ignorant well owner can sell his product and get the same price for it as the most skilful operator. In fact, the trust completely protects them from all the risks of ordinary commerce

and assumes all the reponsibility of the entire industry
itself. The producers, strange to say, seem to be
about as ignorant of the economics of the oil business
as is an ordinary city merchant, imagining that they
are robbed by the arbitrary fixing of the price of the
oil ; they insist that the price is fixed by the trust at
whatever point it pleases.

As a matter of fact, nothing of the kind occurs. If
such were the case, it is needless to say that the trust
would put the price very much lower than it is; practically give nothing for the oil. Crude oil has been as
high as six dollars a barrel. Since the trust was organized the price has been nearly four dollars, frequently
between two and three dollars a barrel. Why does
the trust give nearly three dollars a barrel at one time
and less than seventy cents at another? Why does it
not give seventy cents all the time? The simple answer is that it cannot get the supply at that price.
Despite the trust and all its monopolistic powers, the
price of crude oil is governed by economic conditions
over which neither the well-owners nor the trust have
arbitrary control. Of course, the conditions are different from those in any other industry because the
Standard Oil Company assumes a responsibility which
is assumed by the purchasers of no other commodity.
In no other industry are there either individual or collective interests which stand ready under all circumstances to take the entire product, regardless of the
market demand. This the Standard Oil Company
does, and when there is more than is needed it stores
it, and in so doing it relieves the well owners of all
contingent responsibility. If this were not done, whenever there was more oil produced than was required

the well owners would have to store it or sell at a
sufficiently lower price to pay some one else to store
it.   In that case the price would be governed by the
cost of the dearest portion that the market, under
those competitive conditions, would take, and when
it was too much some would remain unsold.

This competitive element being taken out of the
market by the Standard Oil Company standing ready
to take the entire product causes the economic forces
affecting prices to operate in a different way.   Under
the present arrangement, the trust cannot refuse to
buy when it does not need, hence, when the supply
is greater than the demand and stock is being accumulated, the trust materially lowers the price it will give;
that is to say, it will still take all the product but at
a lower price; and, if the demand is pressing hard
against the supply, it will pay higher prices so as to
induce greater risk in sinking new wells to furnish
an adequate supply.   The trust stands in relation to
crude oil very much as the Bank of England does to
gold.   When it needs a greater supply of gold it raises
the rate of discount; and when there is more than is
needed it lowers the rate of discount, but it always
takes all that comes.   It is thus easy to see that such
an excess of supply would involve a great loss in storage, consequently the Standard offers a lower price.

This is not due to anything the trust does or can do;
it is due to the prolific output of the West Virginia field.
The new wells in West Virginia are each yielding from
one hundred to six hundred barrels a day.   Under the
ordinary competitive conditions of purchase, with such
an output, only what is needed being taken and the
dealers fixing the price, a very large number of single-

barrel wells in Allegany would go out of use because the more prolific wells could supply the whole demand and could lower the price sufficiently to undersell the producers with the small wells. But, since the Standard will take all that is produced, the single-barrel wells can sell their product the same as the six hundred-barrel wells. In other words, the small producers cannot be crowded out by competition, so that in reality it is not the trust that is now fixing the price of oil at seventy-three cents [1] but the prolific wells of Virginia. Thus the law of cost of production operates, despite the seeming monopoly of the purchaser, and operates the same on crude oil as on silver or wheat or any other product. From this there is no final escape, but the well owners in the Allegany fields imagine that because oil was once three and four dollars a barrel and is now only seventy-three cents, therefore the trust has arbitrarily reduced the price by that amount. They seem to know nothing of the economic effect of the West Virginia oil fields on the price of their product. Instead of the trust being the enemy, consciously or otherwise, of the smaller-well owners in Allegany, it is in reality their best and almost only friend, for if the trust were out of the way and free competitive conditions prevailed many of the small-well owners would be driven entirely from the field. For instance, if the one-barrel-well owners had to furnish storage for their own product, transport it themselves and then run the risk of selling it in competition with owners of the more prolific wells, the cost of handling their small amount would be more than the price that they could

---

[1] At present, August 1889, the price of crude oil has gone up to $1.27 per barrel.

get for it. It is only because the trust furnishes all the storage and transportation, and stands ready at all times to buy all the product that these small-well owners can furnish, that they are able to stay in the field at all. As a matter of fact, they are a surplus quantity which competition would drive out; nothing but the economic paternalism of the trust keeps them in existence. Yet curiously enough, it is the small-well owners and not the large ones who think the trust is robbing them.

It is not at all clear, however, that this is a good thing. It is quite certain that in the natural order of competitive evolution a large number of the small-well owners would be rendered economically useless and be eliminated. They would be compelled either to move into the new fields and be a part of the live, active movement, or disappear, but for this somewhat abnormal method of the trust in buying all the product, whether needed or not. It probably would be better for society if they were gradually eliminated by the competitive process, as they would be from farming, manufacture, commerce or any other industry, than to be perpetuated by uneconomic conditions.

The effect of this is clearly seen in the social condition of these economic back-numbers. Under the present system of a guaranteed market for the whole product, oil production is reduced to an almost automatic process. The owner, for instance, of a one-barrel well is as completely assured of remaining in the market as the owner of a six hundred-barrel well. The one-barrel well will yield nearly three hundred dollars a year. This income being guaranteed by the trust against all competition, the owner is relieved from all economic responsibility and resigns himself to a mode of life that will eke out existence on this small income.

Whatever else may be said against the Standard Oil Company, it cannot be charged with crowding out the small producers. On the contrary, it is the only power that perpetuates their existence. Were they exposed to the full force of competition, they would soon be annihilated or compelled to keep pace in the thrifty march of progress. Allentown, Bolivar and Richburg are monuments of industrial sloth and social indifference which are the result of the perpetuation of uneconomic misfits. The effect is bad alike on the individual and the community, without in the least benefiting the industry. The real trouble with oil producers is that they have been shielded by the trust from the normal competitive influence of industrial evolution.

The only remedy for their condition is to apply the same concentration of capital to oil ownership that has taken place in the refining. Instead of the Standard Oil Company giving place to a multitude of small refiners, the true movement would be for the trust or some other similarly large concern to concentrate and organize under one or a few large companies the entire crude oil industry. Then the shiftless hangers-on would be forced into the column of wage workers and the energy and discipline of progressive influences would spur them on to some degree of industrial and social activity. Small-well owners at present are really in the hand labor era of industry, and are lagging behind in the general progress of society through the barbarizing influences that crude life and hand methods always entail.

VII.

TRUSTS *VERSUS* THE TOWN *

Editor Gunton's Magazine:

THE unequivocal industrial tendency to-day is toward the so-called trust. Newspaper notices give almost daily evidence of this fact, and the sharp competition for the world's markets by American manufacturers makes a closer division of labor and a larger investment of capital of first necessity. The most natural thing to do is to form a trust and thereby secure both. That the trust idea is commercially successful needs no demonstration. In fact, where feasible at all, it is the only way open to large success. There is no gainsaying the fact that it is based on the true economic principle and has therefore come to stay, and is the legitimate outcome of its predecessor, the factory system. It is also peculiarly American, and is more nearly an industrial democracy than any other form of commercial institutions. It is democratic because it represents the investments of many, and the many elect the officers who are in control and who for in efficiency or malfeasance may be removed from office. It is democratic because it does not promise any hereditary descent in the control of affairs.

---

* Letter from correspondent, and editorial comment, published in *Gunton's Magazine* of September 1898.

But while we may not ignore this tendency or fail to admit the logic of this is trend, we must look with apprehension on its effect upon the many manufacturing hamlets with which the country is dotted and which so greatly aid the agricultural interests of our eastern and middle states. The trust necessarily seeks a commercial and financial center, a large and wealthy city where it is daily in touch with the pulse of trade and finance. It means, then, abandonment of the smaller factories in the rural towns and withdrawal of the employees who are the tenants of the houses of which the town is built, patrons of the local stores, and consumers of the products of the local farms, leaving the thrifty manufacturing village an empty distributing point for rural necessities which are obviously sold to the farmers at a higher price, while their product is bought at a much lower price on account of the transportation charges anticipated to get it to the consumer.

That this is appreciated by the people is evident from the fact that much investigation into and legislation against trusts is engaging their representatives in the legislatures of the various states, but the immediate effect will not be fully appreciated by those most interested until too late. The trust not only produces an article for less cost than the small manufacturer but it goes farther. It seeks to reduce the cost of distribution by omitting the jobber and in many instances the retail dealer, and selling through its own channels directly to the consumer wherever possible, thus saving to itself the profits of both. By the change then not only the farmer but the country merchant, the country bank, and the village property

holder are all alike menaced. Farmers of the eastern
and middle states have known something of the reduction in land values produced by the opening and operating of large tracts of farm lands in a large way in
the West and South-West, and the cheapened product
therefrom, aided by the improved and cheapened
transportation, but such reduction is only a fraction of what is to come with the industrial changes
now in progress. Those towns which are the happy
possessors of from six to twenty thriving manufacto-
ries employing from 50 to 200 or 300 hands each should
guard them jealously, and the farmers who have derived
thrift therefrom should lend their aid so far as may be
to their maintenance. These factories not only make a
profitable home market, give value to real estate and
thrift and population to a town, but they also pay a
large percentage of the taxes, which would not be not-
ably lessened by their loss but would have to be added
to the burdens of others. How far-reaching the change
will be time will tell, but its effect cannot be doubted.
The town has a fight for self-preservation against the
trust, and should be fully awake to the menace of what
will come if it loses in the contest.

C. D. CHAMBERLIN.

Mr. Chamberlin raises a good point and one that
deserves serious consideration. What he says in regard to the inevitable industrial tendency towards
trusts, and the advantages to come from that movement, is quite in accord with the views of this magazine; nevertheless, it is of great importance that the
growth of towns and cities all through the country, particularly in the great rural sections, shall steadily pro-

ceed, because it is from these centers that the moving forces of progressive civilization radiate. Consequently, if it were true, as Mr. Chamberlin thinks, that the smaller towns and cities are being killed off by the growth of trusts, a serious problem would be presented and some legislative restriction of the trust movement might be justifiable. The question should be looked into thoroughly and discussed with entire fairness.

There is no doubt that the last two decades have witnessed the relative decline of a certain class of small towns in the old-settled portions of the country, chiefly the East. Neither is there any doubt that much of this is chargeable to the modern tendency towards concentration. The beginning of this change was wrought by the railroads. Wherever and as fast as steam transportation took the place of wagons or stages in any given section of the country, the fate of all manufacturing towns not on the line of the road was sealed. Manufacturing, therefore, tended more and more to localize itself along the railroads and the non-railroad towns relapsed into agricultural communities. The next step was a natural continuation of the same movement. Certain kinds of industries can be conducted much more economically and profitably in large establishments than in small; hence, many of the small concerns of this class, even though located on railway lines, found it difficult to compete with the more extensive plants that had naturally grown up in the larger towns and cities, and thus were gradually compelled either to withdraw from business or consolidate and go to larger towns themselves. It is quite true, therefore, that certain lines of industry have been steadily centering in the large towns and cities.

But is this movement chargeable especially to the trust? Not at all. It is due to the general concentrating tendency of which trusts are merely one phase. In fact, the trust integration seldom takes place until after the industries affected by it have already migrated from the villages to the large towns. The railroads and competition of larger concerns were and are responsible for that movement, while the trust is simply an organization of already established concerns and often does not involve changing the location of factories at all. In some cases of course it means closing up the smaller and extending the larger plants, but clearly this is simply a continuation of the earlier movement and is chargeable, not specifically to the trust, but to the entire general trend to which we have referred. The problem therefore becomes a much broader one than that merely of " Trusts *versus* the Town." It expands into the larger question of whether or not the whole modern trend of industry is hindering the multiplication and growth of towns and cities throughout the country.

So far from that being true, the facts show that the trend is exactly the other way. According to the Eleventh Census, the number of cities in the United States increased from 141 in 1860 to 448 in 1890, and of these new communities 187, or 60 per cent., were places of between 8,000 and 20,000 population—hardly more than large towns. The greatest gain of all was in towns of between 8,000 and 12,000 population; these increased from 62 to 176 in the three decades. Cities of from 12,000 to 20,000 population increased from 34 to 107; 20,000 to 40,000, from 23 to 91, and so on. There was only one city of between 500,000 and 1,000,

000 population in 1860, and one in 1890. Not until 1880 were there any cities of over 1,000,000; there was one of that class in 1880, three in 1890.

It is clear, therefore, that the growth in the number of small towns and cities has been pronounced, and that, instead of the small localities being killed off by the larger, it is among these very towns of from 8,000 to 12,000 inhabitants that the principal gain has taken place. The total increase of 307 consisted, of course, of small places which passed from below to above the 8,000 mark during the three decades. All this occurred, it should be remembered, during the period of most marked concentration in industry.

If, however, the growth of railroads and concentration of industry has resulted in the decline of a certain class of small towns, how can this general increase be explained? Chiefly, we believe, by the fact that practically all the decline has been in the case of towns of insignificant population—say of less than 3,000 or 4,000 —and this has been much more than offset by the multiplication and growth of towns of 5,000 to 10,000 and upwards. Thus, if the little industries of a group of small villages should gradually center in one of those villages, the latter would soon become a large town and be included in the census list, while before none of these places would have been recorded either as towns or cities. Hence, in the older sections of the country, for each new town added to the list of places exceeding 8,000 inhabitants there may be two or three or more smaller places left in a static or declining condition. The census statistics for places of from 1,000 to 2,500 population confirm the statement as to the stagnation or decline of very small towns in eastern states.

Throughout the West the case is different. There small towns and large (except the " boom towns " of a few years ago) are steadily growing. Most of these places have come into existence since the new conditions of concentrated industry were established and hence are making use of instead of suffering by these conditions. Only such industries as are capable of success in relatively small places are being located in the towns of the West, and that region is not being built up with thousands of little agricultural communities, as was done in the East before the modern industrial era came in. Thus, while some of the small towns of the West may, hereafter, recede before their stronger neighbors, the movement cannot possibly be so widespread and significant as it has been throughout the old states of New England and the Atlantic seaboard.

There is every indication, however, that towns of 5,000 to 10,000 and upwards will continue to thrive and increase in number. In the first place, while many lines of industry must be carried on, nowadays, in large establishments, it does not follow that such concerns will tend to locate themselves in very large cities ; indeed, to avoid heavy taxation and rent they tend more and more to seek towns and cities of moderate size. Good railroad facilities make this possible, and thus we see that while railroads were at first the means of drawing village industries into larger towns, they are now becoming the strongest force to keep such industries from going into the great cities. Moreover, the economic tendency is and will be more and more for manufacturing industries to locate themselves near the sources of raw material, because transportation of finished commodities is relatively much more economical than of bulky raw products containing a great amount of waste. This means that manufacturing will steadily diffuse itself throughout the country, according to the geographical distribution of natural resources; while the very large cities will become more exclusively mercantile, commercial, financial and general distributive centers.

Look wherever we will the facts confirm this theory. Most of the manufacturing in New England, of cotton and woolen goods, boots and shoes, paper, cutlery, bicycles, etc., except in Massachusetts and Rhode Island, is carried on in towns of from 5,000 to 25,000 inhabitants; and, in the two excepted states even, in places of less than 50,000 or 75,000. The cotton industry is going South, near the raw cotton; woolen manufacture will eventually move westward, near the raw wool; in both cases establishing industrial communities in those sections. Iron is manufactured near the iron mines, furniture (very much of it) near the forests of Michigan, flour near the wheatfields of Minnesota, raw sugar on the plantations. In time, most of the refining of sugar will undoubtedly be done near the sources of its production.

Another important fact. New industries are continually coming into existence, and the vast majority of these establish themselves in relatively small towns or cities, because they cannot begin on a sufficiently large scale to command success in a large city. Some of these may finally move to the cities, but, with the progress of invention, still other enterprises are continually being established, and may be counted upon as a permanent reliance of the small town.

Thus from every point of view the steady multiplication and prosperity of most towns and cities of from 5,000 and 10,000 population upwards, seems to be assured. Villages, especially in the East, which have not reached that point and cannot reach it, will probably remain static or decline. Since their places are being taken by an increasing number of larger centers, this decline of small villages need not necessarily be considered a calamity. From a sentimental or a local standpoint it may perhaps be deplored, but the nation's interest is not in the mere preservation of little crossroads hamlets but in the increase and distribution of communities sufficiently large and complex to exert a genuine socializing influence on its inhabitants and the surrounding country. It is hardly possible to get much of this influence in a place of less than 10,000 inhabitants; with a smaller number there is not enough complexity of interests, variety of ideas and social intercourse, nor a sufficient basis for first-class educational facilities and public improvements. The drawing together of industries, therefore, in such a way as to increase the number of moderately large towns and small cities is an advantage to the whole country, even if the small villages do cease to be centers of industry and trade.

But it is not to be assumed that the small villages will be entirely wiped out, even though many of them may lose a part of their population. Certain kinds of industries will always be found in these small villages, such as lumber and planing mills, grist mills, barrel factories, cheese and fruit-canning factories, creameries, carriage shops, and repairing establishments of various kinds. Many of these villages, also, will probably be transformed into residence places, educational centers and summer resorts,—witness the fine old towns of New England. Others will form the *nuclei* of future agricultural towns, in which the farmers will live and go out to their work every day. Improvement of country roads and more general use of farm machinery, permitting shorter hours of labor, will contribute to this result ; eventually, the trolley will probably be used for this purpose, just as it is now employed to take city workers into suburban districts at night.

The modern trend of industry is producing two distinct results—cheaper wealth and higher wages; in other words, increased consuming power of the masses of the people. This increased consuming power means a larger effective demand for the products of industry —hence more factories and more factory towns. Trusts do not affect new industries at first, and many kinds of manufacturing are never reached by the trust at all, because no economy would result. These combinations occur in certain kinds of long-established industries, but the factories themselves, even when consolidated in a few great plants, are not necessarily located in large cities. High taxes and remoteness from raw materials operate against that movement. There is no ground for supposing that trusts are proving or will prove inimical to the small towns and cities of the country. On the contrary, the concentration tendency, with the natural balancing checks we have mentioned, is directly contributing to the increase of that class of communities whose influence is a powerful stimulative factor in the social progress of the nation.

VIII.

THE STATE'S RELATION TO CAPITAL *

THE lack of general recognition on the part of capitalists of the legitimacy of organized labor is the cause of much antagonism between labor and the employing class. Laborers act unwisely sometimes, and their occasional unwisdom is made to stand for their entire conduct, and this mistaken attitude towards the laboring class as a distinct element in the community is developing a severe and dangerously acrimonious class feeling between the laborers and their employers. This extends to practically every class in the community, and not the least to the professional classes, who are governed largely by abstract ideas and sentiments, and hence a social atmosphere antagonistic to capital is created by the mistaken attitude of capitalists themselves toward the labor question.

The opposition to labor organizations by the employing class is largely due to the failure of the employing class and of public educators correctly to understand the new conditions created by the revolutionary industrial progress that has taken place during the last half century. What is true of capital towards labor in this respect is eminently true of labor and the community towards capital. The conditions which have so altered

* Lecture delivered in New York City, October 18, 1898.

the character of industry during the last fifty years, and particularly during the last twenty-five years, have created as much of a revolution in the conditions and character of capitalist enterprise as it has in laborers' conditions. Forty years ago a capitalist with one hundred thousand dollars was nearly at the top of the ladder of industrial enterprise, and was among the leaders of the best methods and most efficient type of organization; but, with the development of new devices and the application of new inventions, machinery has undergone such an enormous change that the methods of twenty years ago are effete and impotent for aught but loss to-day, and real organization of productive industrial methods has become absolutely necessary to ordinary success. A hundred thousand dollars is scarcely enough to run a small mercantile establishment now. Nothing short of millions is adequate to efficient productive enterprise in most of the great established industries of the country. This large capital and organization is made necessary by the intricacy of the new devices. The new methods which work so much more efficiently and cheaply than the old are available only when production can be maintained on a large scale. The improved features involve specialization of each department, interdependent with other departments, so that unless the whole can be conducted on a colossal scale the advantages of the new devices cannot be obtained. It is on the plan that to carry a small number of people a railroad would be dearer and more expensive than a stage coach; yet, when hundreds of thousands ride every day, the Manhattan Railroad can carry us ten miles for five cents, and the surface railroad even a greater distance; whereas, if only those who had incomes of ten to twenty thousand a year should ride they could go the same distance cheaper in a coach and four. It is only when the service can be utilized by the millions that the results are cheaper by the new than by the old methods.

This revolution has entered almost every domain of industry. It is very natural that in this transition and reorganization the small concerns and individual enterprises conducted on the old and highly expensive methods should have to succumb. They are superseded by the new in exactly the same manner that the hand loom was superseded by the power loom, the stage coach by the railroad, the tallow candle by gas, and now by electricity. This is inevitable, but it always follows, and probably always will, that the defeated complain; that those who cannot keep up with the rest complain at the unfairness of the others for going so fast. There is nothing unnatural in this; indeed, it is in the nature of things. The consequence is that in the last quarter of a century this superseding of one type by another and supplanting of one method of production by another has produced a great deal of this resentment in the community. The feeling of hardship among those who are thus being displaced is not that the successful men are capitalists, because it is a case of capitalist superseding capitalist. It is just the same among laborers. The hand-loom weavers smashed the machines and mobbed their fellow laborers who used the power looms;—not because they were capitalists, or of another class, for they were all weavers, but one was using new methods which seemed to be endangering the possibility of survival of the old.

This tendency of concentration and integration of

capital to bear hard on the smaller concerns is not because they are essentially different but because the new capitalist is superseding the old capitalist. In each case there is a tendency to cry out: "Unfairness," and sometimes there is unfairness. The wail of complaint from this class of defeated competitors has taken form in an appeal to the public for raising the hand of the state against the growth of capitalist aggregations. The cry of monopoly, which is always a note of alarm, is vigorously utilized, and the public is asked to use the political power of the state to suppress this ever increasing capitalist tendency. With the feeling that exists towards capitalists and the employing class, particularly among the laborers, a ready ear is offered to every such complaint.

The history of the last ten years shows that the legislation in almost every state in the Union has a very strong anti-capital flavor. It is almost a commonplace that a person to run for public office must be against trusts, or must in some way or another express his willingness to enact legislation to repress the action of large corporations. Only last evening Tammany Hall held its great send-off meeting in the gubernatorial campaign of this state, and it brought upon the platform, for the purpose of oratorical and political effect, ex-Governor Campbell, of Ohio. Mr. Campbell proclaimed, loudly and with seeming seriousness, that the republican party was the party of trusts, the party of large corporations, and appealed to the voters to sustain the democratic nominees because they were opposed to corporate enterprises. Any one who knows Mr. Campbell knows that this was political gush, mere demagogy—a specimen of the worst kind of political

humbug.   Mr. Campbell is one of the conspicuous instances of a man who makes his living largely by organ-
izing new corporations.   He gets big bonuses and
large fees and what are called " ground-floor interests "
in large corporations for the service he renders in or-
ganizing these institutions.   When, therefore, he appeals to the voters of New York city and state to support a certain party because it is the enemy of these
organizations, he is a mere public humbug.   He does
not believe what he says, but he talks to stimulate
public prejudice on the subject, merely for the purpose
of catching votes for the immediately ensuing election.

   This is dangerous business, but it is becoming more
and more general.   The people who indulge in this
sort of talk act largely upon the belief that all that is
necessary is to humbug the people during the campaign, and then ignore them after the election is over.
They hope to avoid carrying out their promises by the
practise of the doctrine that platforms are made to
get in on, not to stand on.   But this dishonesty, which
much of it is, takes real hold.   Though Mr. Campbell
does not believe the stuff that he talked, many of his au-
dience did.   The people are more honest than the demagogues, and take them at their word.   They believe in
this anti-capitalist idea, because it has become a part
of this kind of irresponsible public propaganda.   The
consequence is that when such a man as Mr. Campbell
is elected governor he cannot altogether withstand the
demands of the legislators whom his audiences have
elected, and, though he may not believe in it, he is forced
to acquiesce in repressive legislation against capital
and thus handicap the industrial development of the
country.   Not to do this creates a furious agitation.

The press, a certain portion of which is as demagogical as are the Crokers and Campbells, appeals to the laborers and to every victim of social misfortune on the same line, until the atmosphere becomes surcharged with a sort of quasi-socialism.

This leads to a perversion of the action of the state towards capital, which some day may be found to have so completely harassed the action of capital that our industrial progress will be seriously retarded and perhaps even brought to a halt. A conspicuous instance of the way in which this perverted public opinion is created is the case of the Standard Oil Company. That is the largest and perhaps the most successful trust in the country. It has been eminently successful in improving the quality and cheapening the cost of the commodity it produces. In doing this, as is generally the case, it has been exceptionally prosperous, as it should be. That form of enterprise which does things best and does them cheapest ought to be most successful, else improvements would not go on ; and that which does things the poorest and charges the most for the same product ought not to succeed, since to do so would practically be to put a premium on incapacity and put improvement to a disadvantage.

The Standard Oil Company has been the object of more abuse and legislative attack, because of its conspicuous success, than any other corporation. Legislation has been introduced in the United States congress to check what is called " trust organization." Even Senator Sherman was caught by the clamor and became the instrument of this sentiment, and introduced what is known as the " Sherman Anti-trust Law." Several states have enacted legislation for the object of crippling or forcing the Standard Oil organization into dissolution, for no other reason than that the clamor against it has entered into the domain of politics and affected the political opinion of the community.

Last week a public hearing was held at the New Amsterdam Hotel in New York City, in the case of the State of Ohio against the Standard Oil Company. As a result of the sentiment to which I have referred, Ohio passed a law demanding that the Standard Oil Company of Ohio sever its connection with the Standard Oil trust, and, as the process of dissolution has not been complete, the anti-capital agitators operating in politics in Ohio sent a special delegation representing the Supreme Court of Ohio to conduct an investigation into the subject in this city. I attended one of these public hearings and met a man by the name of George Rice, from Marietta; in the company of the counsel for the State of Ohio. Upon my asking for the room where the hearing was to be conducted, the counsel for Ohio asked if I represented any paper. I said no, I represented *Gunton's Magazine.* "Oh yes," said Mr. Rice, "that magazine has been saying hard things about me." And then, as I suppose is typical of the character of the man, he broke out into a line of profane abuse which cannot be repeated here. I told him that I had said in the magazine that I believed him to be a bold blackmailer; I still believed it, and had come specially to hear what he could say on the stand. To my surprise, this man of more than six feet suddenly became calm and docile and proceeded to assure me that he was in the habit of telling the truth! During the conversation I reminded him of the fact that he had for years been making a business of pursuing the Standard Oil Company to compel it to give him half a million dollars for property that nobody would give him twenty-five thousand for, and that because they would not buy at his absurd price he had been pursuing them in all legal and political ways for fifteen or twenty years. He promised to call at my office with the evidence which should convince me of his innocence, but he has not done so.

A few days after, in the line of his usual methods, he got himself interviewed by the New York *World*, which published his statement with a half-page picture in last Sunday's edition, printing part of his interview in full faced black type, and embellishing the story with adjectives and emphasis, presenting him to the public as a martyr of this cruel system of large organizations, and particularly of the Standard Oil Company.

Now, the public has no benefit to derive from corporations unfairly getting the upper hand of competitors by uneconomic methods, but, on the other hand, it has no interest in coddling and encouraging blackmailers to beset successful business men and, in case of failure, to threaten them with adverse legislation or with adverse judicial decisions. This Rice case is perhaps one of the most conspicuous of its kind in the country, and has been made the most of, and since it is now revamped by other " yellow " journals as well as the *World*, I think it is worth while here to say a little specifically on its merits. I do not wish to imply that there are many George Rices, but inasmuch as this is made a basis of almost national appeal to the public to legislate against corporations and against capital, on the ground of this man's innocent "martyrdom," it may be well to puncture a little of the fraud and humbug connected with his particular case.

I will take only a few of his statements in this interview. Of course, his general assertion is that the railroads are all in league with the Standard Oil Company to crush such as he. It is a little peculiar, anyhow, that the whole organized railroad capital in the community should go into a conspiracy against such an innocent and harmless creature as Mr. Rice represents himself to be.

His first specific indictment is that the railroads carry oil for the Standard Oil Company cheaper than they will for him. This is done, he says, by the railroads refusing to furnish tank cars and compelling jobbers to ship in barrels or box cars, while the Standard Oil Company has built tank cars for itself, which the railroads haul for nothing. That is to say, when the independent shippers send oil to the Pacific seaboard they are charged $105, he says, to return the empty cylinder tank car from the Pacific to the Missouri River. These tank cars of the Standard Oil Company, he says, are returned for nothing, thus giving the trust an advantage of $100 a car over such as he. This sounds plausible, and it would be a hardship if it were true. But the facts in the case are that there is only one railroad in the country that will build tank cars, because their business will not warrant the investment. That road is the Pennsylvania. The Pennsylvania Railroad has a terminus in the oil fields and at the seaboards, and therefore has more through traffic of that kind than any other road, and can afford to invest in tank cars. The Pennsylvania Railroad supplies these cars to every independent producer on exactly the same terms that it furnishes them to the Standard Oil Company, and Mr. Rice does not venture to state to the contrary. But Mr. Rice refused to take advantage of this, and never built any tank cars himself. He continued the old crude method of shipping in barrels, and was therefore naturally at a disadvantage with those who shipped in tank cars, just the same as the manufacturer who insists upon using old effete machinery will be at a disadvantage with the one who uses the new, most modern inventions. The Standard Oil Company has done another thing. It has had many of its own tank cars so constructed that they can be used to transport freight on their return, thus being able to earn something both ways. When the railroads can use the tank cars to bring return freight, the Standard Oil Company is not charged for the hauling. Why should it be? But when they are brought back empty it has to pay exactly the same as anybody else ; so that Mr. Rice's statement on that point is simply false. It is simply a sour-minded misrepresentation of the facts in the case. The next point he makes is that the railroads make vile discriminations in favor of the Standard Oil Company and permit it to ship oil in small quantities at the rate that is charged for full cars, which privilege it does not extend to other shippers. On this point Mr. Rice says :

"Yet another thing helped to ruin me. The railroads allowed the trust to deliver its oil in less than carload quantities at the same rates as for full carloads. They allowed the trust to stop its cars, whether carrying oil in bulk or barrels, at different stations and take it off in small quantities without paying the higher rates which independent competitors were always charged for small quantities thus delivered. Of course, against such discriminations as these the independent competitor of moderate capital could not contend. He was driven to the wall every time, as I was."

Here is another instance that, if true, would indeed be grossly unfair. But the facts in this case, as Mr. Rice well knows, do not sustain his statement. He has been before the Inter-State Commerce Commission with this complaint; it was thoroughly investigated and proven not to be true in a single instance. The decision on this point is reported in the case of Rice versus Railroad Companies, Fifth Inter-State Commerce Commission Report, page 660. Here is what the Commission says on the point:

"The third ground of complaint appears to be wholly unfounded. There is no evidence that ' favored ' shippers have secured carload rates on less than carload shipments, by being permitted to remove portions of the contents of cars at intermediate stations between the points of shipment and of destination. The verified answers of the defendants explicitly deny that any such discriminations have occurred and that denial is fortified by the positive testimony of their witnesses. The petitioner did not appear at the hearing, though duly notified thereof, and has offered no proof in support of the information and belief upon which his allegations were made. As to these charges the complaint must be dismissed."

Thus you see this man Rice labored to get this complaint before the Inter-State Commerce Commission, and then, after being duly notified, had not the courage to appear, and the thing was thoroughly investigated and his allegations proved to be untrue in every particular. Yet in the face of this decision he expresses himself before the public in this specially imposing interview, and asserts that this thing is still true. He repeats what he knows, and what the Inter-State Commerce Commission has declared, to be absolutely and unqualifiedly unfounded.

I ought to have said that his statement that the Standard Oil Company gets its empty tank cars returned free has also been the subject of investigation by the Inter-State Commerce Commission, and in that case again the charge was found to be wholly unsupported. Rice could give no evidence of the truth of his affirmation, yet he repeats it in this demagogical way as if it were a verified fact, when he knows it is a literally false statement.

Another statement that Mr. Rice made in this interview was regarding the so-called " South Improvement Company," and that there may be no mistake I will read what he says :—

" To understand the growth of this crushing monopoly you need to go back to the foundation of it. In January, 1872, the trunk lines of railroads made a contract with a corporation called ' The South Improvement Company,' which was only another name for the Standard Oil Company, under which the Standard Oil Company was allowed the most outrageous discriminating freight rates. It seems incredible that these contracts should have been made. They not only gave the Standard Oil Company heavy rebates on their own shipments of oil, but gave them rebates on the shipments of their competitors. At that time the

Standard Oil Company only had 10 per cent. of the petroleum industry of the country, while their competitors had 90 per cent.   The rebates allowed to the Standard people were from 40 cents to $1.06 per barrel on crude petroleum, and from 50 cents to $1.32 per barrel on refined petroleum.   Thus the Standard Oil Company received nine times as much for rebates on the shipments of its competitors as it did on its own."

This is a fair sample of what might properly be characterized as the villainy of this man's method of procedure.   You remember that a few years ago (1894) a man named Lloyd published a book called "Wealth against Commonwealth," and he made a statement similar to this.   I investigated the matter at the time and found out (and have since discovered that Mr. Lloyd knew it) that this "South Improvement Company" never had any existence at all; that it was a pure myth.   All there was of it was that a few men met together and got up a scheme which was so bad that they never dared for one moment to try to put it into practise.   This man Rice speaks of it, Mr. Lloyd spoke of it, and hundreds of other people who hear these statements continue to speak of it as though it were a *bona fide* company which actually did business with the railroads and got these fabulous rebates. Now, Mr. Rice knows, or he ought to know before he speaks as a martyr authority on the subject, that this so-called "South Improvement Company" never did a dollar's worth of business in the world, and therefore not one penny of these rebates was ever paid, because the whole thing was a still-born affair; yet he repeats that lie as if it were veritable truth to-day.

Undoubtedly, in the seventies, the railroads did give

rebates to the Standard Oil Company, but in no such way as the mythical contract of the South Improvement Company indicates. In talking about rebates it should be remembered that at that time it was the habit of all railroads to give rebates to large shippers. It was not peculiar to the Standard Oil Company, nor to any other large shipper. They gave rebates in the same way and for the same reason that purchasers of large quantities can always get a better price than the purchasers of small quantities. The Standard Oil Company was a very large shipper, and the railroads wanted its trade, and they bid, just as paper manufacturers or producers in any line will bid, for the trade of a very large customer and one whose payment is prompt and sure.

It is on the same principle as the long and short-haul matter, in the case of railroads. Anybody who knows anything of railroading knows that if the same rate were paid per mile for all freight on long distances, on many of the roads a large portion of their territory would be absolutely excluded from reaching the market. It is not only customary, but it is definitely economic and good business, for a railroad to take freight under some circumstances at less than it would actually cost if the investment and rolling stock were all considered. When a road is equipped, all its fixed costs are substantially the same to do a small business as to do a large one. Indeed, traffic obtained in this way frequently enables a road to lower freight on its whole business; yet those who do not get the lower, or long-haul, rates think they are injured and cry out against it. As a matter of fact they are benefited, because without the long-haul business the rates on the short-haul would have to be higher in order to make the road pay at all. That is the secret of all rebates for large business, or great discounts for large orders and cash payments. There is nothing exceptional in the rebate idea for large business. It is as old and as permanent as business itself.

Another statement that this man makes is in regard to a railroad scheme for carrying oil from Macksburg to Marietta. On this point he says—I again use his own words :—

"To show you how the rebate system worked in my own case, let me say that in 1885 I was charged 35 cents a barrel for carrying oil from Macksburg to Marietta, a distance of twenty-five miles, while the Standard Oil Company paid only 10 cents a barrel for the same distance. More than this, out of the 35 cents a barrel that I paid the trust actually received 25 cents. In other words, the trust received about two-thirds of all the money I paid for freight."

This, you observe, he presents as one of the things that helped to ruin him. The facts in this case have been brought out fully in the public hearings and in the courts, but Mr. Rice knows that the average reader of newspapers has not read these investigations and court reports, and therefore he feels perfectly safe to go on making a repeated announcement of this alleged piece of infamy. The facts in this case are these : At the time to which he refers the railroad company mentioned was, I believe, in the hands of a receiver. Some local agent of the Standard Oil Company made a contract with the railroad with some such features as Mr. Rice here describes, though not exactly, but at any rate the contract was an outrageous one. The agreement

8

was enforced immediately, before it was submitted to the trust at all. As soon as it reached headquarters it was seen to be obviously not merely unfair but illegal, and was revoked and the transaction stopped; and what is more, *every dollar of overcharge that had been collected was returned.* Mr. Rice, by reason of that transaction, had paid in overcharge (all this was brought out in the public hearings) something over two hundred dollars, and it was all returned to him; so that, bad as the contract was, Mr. Rice never lost a penny by it. For him to present that as one of the ways by which he was ruined only reveals the character of the man.

I refer to this particular case, as I said, because it is just now being made a conspicuous illustration of the heartless, crushing and deadening influence of great corporations, particularly the Standard Oil Company, and this man is paraded as a typical victim. But, it may be asked, what motive has he for doing all this? This is a very proper question. The motive has been thoroughly revealed in the various attempts Mr. Rice has made in trying to get decisions and legislation against the Standard Oil Company. The secret of it is that he wants to blackmail the Standard Oil Company out of a half a million of dollars. The simple facts on that aspect of the case, which I repeated to Mr. Rice's face and which he has not kept his promise to furnish the evidence against, are about like this:

He was a small refiner in Marietta. He did not keep up with the current of improvements and made up his mind that he would sell his plant instead of adopting the new methods, such as building tank cars, and other improvements. He decided that he would try to force the Standard Oil Company to buy his property at a fabulous price. The property was worth at one time perhaps about twenty-five thousand dollars, but with the neglect and lack of up-to-date appliances is worth practically nothing to-day. He went to the Standard Oil Company (and this has been in evidence in the courts) and wanted to sell out for a half a million of dollars. They declined to buy. One would think that if a person had a piece of property to sell and he tried to sell it to a party and they declined to buy, he would go and search other purchasers, or use the property himself. But no; this man made up his mind that he would make them buy, and if they would not buy he would make it cost them a good deal more than half a million, and it is for not buying it at this price that he has pursued them and devoted as much energy to trying to compel, by fair means or foul, the Standard Oil Company to give him half a million dollars for his plant, as would, by application to his industry, have probably earned him twice that amount. It often happens that lazy people will put forth more energy not to do a thing than is required to do it. This appears to be Mr. Rice's case. He has pursued the Standard Company during all these years, and accompanied his propositions with threats that if they did not come to terms he would instigate hostile legislation, *etc.* I exposed this matter two or three years ago in an interview given the *Boston Herald*, in reply to an interview on the subject by Mr. Lloyd, to whom I have already referred. Since that time this man Rice has repeated his propositions to the Standard Oil Company, directly and indirectly, several times. He is getting very cunning, to be sure, and refuses to put much in writing. Sometimes he has sent irresponsible brokers, with whom, doubtless, he promised to divide the spoils. Sometimes he has succeeded in getting a reputable lawyer to approach the trust with his proposition. Recently he did this, and the company refused to talk unless the lawyer could furnish written authority for his action, and he did so, and, when asked what Mr. Rice had to sell or deliver for the five hundred thousand dollars he was demanding as a stand-up price, he gave a schedule of property worth less than ten thousand dollars, but frankly said that the greater part of the value he had to deliver was the withdrawal of litigation, the stopping of further annoyance, and the heading off of an adverse decision by the Inter-State Commerce Commission. Rice actually attempted to trade by this blackmailing method upon his power to influence legislation and the decisions of the Inter-State Commerce Commission.

I did not intend to dwell so long upon this case, but it is being made so much of and is so scandalous that I could not refrain from speaking of it. It is not an average case, I am glad to say, but it is at least a case which shows the lengths to which a perverted sentiment against capital may go. The encouragement that this man has received by demagogical newspapers and public clamor is the thing which alone has sustained him in his highwayman methods.

It is time that public sentiment was aroused on this subject. We are in danger of suffering quite as much from this false and pernicious attitude, and the consequent legislation, as we are from the rash conduct of illy-informed and demagogically-led labor mobs. Labor has its legitimate rights, and the state has a true function and duty towards laborers, as I have said, which is educational and protective. The protection should always be in the rigid guarding of every right laborers have acquired, and in the maximum assistance to every new opportunity, social, industrial and political, that the laborers can, either individually or in their organized capacity, take advantage of. In reference to capital the same is true. There are capitalists who will wantonly oppress labor and who will wantonly, if needs be, corrupt the state. But this is not the general character of American business men, any more than demagogy is the general character of American laborers.

There is no one thing that is more dangerous to public welfare than this unwholesome, chiefly unfounded, and perverted antagonism to the legitimate development of capital into corporate forms and large enterprises. The state should permit the free movement of this tendency, for it is through this progress alone that the community, of which laborers constitute a large majority, get the real benefits of modern civilization; —the cheaper wealth, the shorter working day, the new devices for domestic and social improvement, the great public expenditures, improvements in domestic architecture, and so on, all of which are the outcome of capitalistic development. Take away concentration of capital, so that millions cannot be devoted to experimentation, as now; give us small concerns with a few hundred thousand dollars capital, and we are at once put back to the relatively simple life and plodding methods of fifty years ago. Take away concentrated capital and we take the very life-blood of industrial, social and political progress out of the community. The improved efficiency and organization of productive forces are essential to modern progress. What we want, and what the state must be utilized to give us, is protection and freedom for the productive forces of society, because it is only by this superior application of capital that any increased contribution to the community's aggregate wealth can come, and it is on this increased contribution to the aggregate wealth of the community that the only hope of the laborers for betterment of their condition really rests.

At the same time let us see to it that labor has the encouragement of the state in every legitimate means that it can devise to take an increasing portion of the products of this capital and transfer it to the wage-earners and the public. The true way in which this can be done (and must be done if it is done at all) is not by legislation against capital, not by socialization of industry, not by public control, but by increasing the social and political influences by which wages shall be increased, hours of labor reduced, and public improvements made. It is only by these means that the laborers can get an addition to their income or a contribution to superior social conditions. But in order that the condition of the laborers may be improved in these ways, that their organized efforts may be efficient in demanding higher wages, better social conditions, greater freedom and opportunity, we must at the same time protect and encourage the possibilities of the source from which this wealth is to be taken, *viz.*, capitalistic production. Any organized effort to use the state against the free development and application of science and organization to industry is a movement against public welfare, against the laborer, against progress and against civilization.

IX.

THE STATE'S RELATION TO LABOR *

In discussing the relation of the state to labor, it is not a question of whether the state can do this or that, but whether it ought to do this or that, and the ought to do and wisdom of doing must not and cannot be determined by mere feeling, or the seeming immediate necessity or local emergency. It should be governed by the general principle of what in the light of economic science and experience is most likely in the long run to promote the welfare of the laboring class. As I have frequently remarked, the functions of the state are primarily protective, educational and judiciary; that is, to protect the interests and rights of society, to adjudicate competing claims between parties, and to promote in all the ways feasible the educational influences and opportunities among the people, with the view of developing a more intelligent standard of citizenship and a broader social character in the community. In this respect the duty of the state, it will be seen, is not directly to do for the people, as, for instance, in giving employment and running industries and owning property or conducting in any way profit-making enterprises; but rather to exercise its supreme authority in the direction of guarding and increasing

---

* Lecture delivered in New York City, October 11th, 1898.

the opportunities for self-improvement in every domain of life among the citizens. This, in a simple society, may involve very little state action, but as society grows in complexity and diversity the number of ways in which the state can act in fulfilling its educational functions steadily multiplies, and the multiplication of these activities may seem at first sight like making the state more paternal, when in reality it is only extending the action of the state to new protective needs or educational opportunities which the new conditions and interests have created.

This is conspicuously the case in reference to the labor question. When industry was conducted by simple methods, and the majority of the people worked for themselves or were employed in simple industries like agriculture and hand manufacture, the problems were simple and the functions of the state in relation to labor were very meager. They consisted chiefly of providing for the care of paupers, insane, and otherwise helpless members of the community; in the normal conditions of employment there was little for the state to do, because there was but little complexity and few new interests and problems. With the growth of modern industry, however, since the completion of the factory system, this has radically changed. In no sphere of society has the expansion and multiplication of interests and problems been so great as among the wage class. This is very natural. The development of steam, and of capitalistic methods of industry, revolutionized the entire type of industry, methods of working, and social life of the laboring class. It transformed the laborer from an individual producer to a fractional economic automaton. It made the shoemaker into a peg driver, a sole cutter, or any one of more than sixty sub-divisions of shoemaking. It did the same with the weaver and spinner and every mechanic employed in complex machine-using manufacture.

This is not to be lamented. It is not something which should be got rid of, or against which society should be organized and public sentiment inflamed and the hand of the state adversely raised ; but it is a fact to be recognized, it is the process by which modern civilization has come. It is the process by which western civilization must be taken to the East. It is the process, in short, by which barbarism shall be eliminated and an ever higher and higher civilization ushered in and established. Consequently, it is a fact to be recognized and reckoned with, and not fought and denounced.

By "recognition" of this fact in its full significance I mean more than merely to know that it is here ; I mean, recognize it as being here to stay, and being here as in reality the only means of promoting a higher state of civilization. Consequently this should not be in any sense made the basis of any policy of subversion or overthrow, but should be recognized and studied solely with the view of adapting society to it. To resist it is like resisting the law of gravitation.

This means that we must recognize as a thing inevitably to be counted with that the laboring class as a class has ceased to be composed of what we like to call independent individuals. The laborer is not economically an individual. He has not the freedom to make

individual contracts. He cannot, if he would, go to an
employer and stipulate for himself alone the wages he
shall have, the hours of labor he shall work, and the
specific conditions under which he shall work. The
capitalist could not, if he would, grant or concede
special contracts with each individual laborer on these
matters. The very nature of employment has made it
impossible. The great factory methods have made the
organization of production inevitable, by which all
laborers in a given industry must work under common
conditions as to hours of labor, wages and sanitary
conditions of various kinds. This is no longer at the
individual option of either the employer or the laborer.
Then it is useless, it is futile, it is false, longer to talk
of the laborer as having the right, even relatively, to
make individual contracts regarding all these primary
conditions of earning a living.

This has necessarily reduced the laborers to an industrial group or class. Bricklayers are a group.
They must act in common or not at all. Carpenters,
weavers, shoemakers, tailors, are groups; they are
parts of an industrial man, not complete industrial individuals. They never can be that without returning
to the simple methods of hand labor and relative barbarism. It is not important that they should be industrial individuals, but it is important that the fact that
they are not should be recognized, and therefore that
the individualist idea be not urged against them when
they are naturally acting in groups. In acting in groups
and organized unions they do a great many things
which are indefensible, as do all groups. In that sense
they are not exceptions. All social organizations make
mistakes, have bad leaders, ignorant representatives,

demagogues,—in short, unscrupulous and inefficient members who sometimes get to the front.   This is true of church organizations, social organizations, political organizations, and so on.   Our political bossism, against which public warfare is now so rife, is a conspicuous instance of the kind.   In dealing with this particular phase of the labor question, which is a pressing one because it comes up most frequently, we make the maximum amount of mistakes.   The reasoning on the subject by populists, legislators and most economists is painful in its lack of recognition of the fact that the defects of the labor movement are defects of a natural movement.   The tendency all the time is to insist that the movement is unnatural.   Here the economic textbooks are as much to blame as any other kind of contribution to public sentiment on the subject.   It is quite common for economists and for editors, theorists and intelligent leaders of public opinion to censure the labor movement because its promoters are only a part of the whole labor body.

In a work on *The Political Economy of Natural Law*, the author, Henry Wood, takes great pains to show that the despotism and oppressive features of the trade union movement consist in the fact that its membership never includes more than a small minority of the whole wage class for which it pretends to speak.   I mention this because this writer states what has almost become hackneyed,—as though it were a conclusive answer to the claim of the legitimacy of organized labor.   Trade unions, on this theory, have no right to speak for the laboring class unless their membership includes at least a majority of the class.   On this principle there is not a political party, nor a church, nor an organization of any kind that would have a right to speak. If we say that trade unions do not represent the interests and sentiments of their class, because their membership roll does not contain a majority of the members of the class, we might say that the churches do not represent the Christian sentiment of the community, for surely it is true that the membership roll of the churches does not include anywhere near a majority of the whole community. We might say that the republican or democratic party does not represent the republicans and democrats in any community because the membership roll of the organization does not contain a majority of the voters of that political faith in that community. By that test there could be no party, for in no district, certainly in no crowded district, does the party organization include a majority of the party voters in that community. This argument is contrary to all human experience in group action.

Representation seldom includes a majority of the whole, never the whole. The truth is that representation in voluntary organizations includes the active spirits who voice the sentiments silently acquiesced in by the rest. The idea that the organization does not represent a body because its membership rolls do not include the majority of those interested has no experience whatever to rest upon. It is a sophistical quibble. It is the invention of the sophist in special pleading against the laborers, and is applied to no other form of social or economic or political organization. It is wholly unwarranted, and in justice to the laborers it should be discarded. In no other form of organization that I know of do we exact perfection on the penalty of disorganization. We do not think of asking, for instance, that political organizations and political parties shall be renounced and abolished because they occasionally run into corruption, as in the case of Tammany, and develop objectionable bosses here and there, in the form of leaders. Not at all. Nobody asks that the Christian Church should be abolished because now and then a vestryman or a minister conducts himself in a manner unbecoming a Christian. No. In all other spheres the idea is accepted that there must be reforms, that the methods must be improved, that the membership be elevated, that the leadership be purified. But the defects in labor organizations are all cited to show the unnaturalness and the unfeasibility of the organization itself. In short, the shortcomings are cited to show that unions *per se* are an injury.

It must be admitted that there is a tendency to outgrow this narrow view of the subject; that in spite of all this kind of reasoning the unions stay, workingmen organize, and go on as if nothing had been said at all. The very fact of their existence and increasing influence is forcing itself upon public recognition; but so long as in theory we hold the idea that these organizations are bad, unnatural, uneconomic, and contrary to the best interests of society and the best interests of the laborers themselves, we shall continue to regard them from the wrong point of view,—from the point of view of suppressing rather than improving them. So long as we do that, we encourage the hostile attitude of the employing class and the hostile attitude of the representatives of society towards this great movement, and hostility always tends to pervert any real, helpful reform attitude. So long as we think

a thing is bad we see only bad in it, and seek to abolish it instead of recognizing that in itself, at the core,
it is all right and only needs improving in its methods
and character. This makes all the difference in how
we see and therefore how we treat the subject.

This very mistake has more to do with the angry
conflicts between organized labor and organized capital than any other one thing. It begets the spirit
among the laborers on the one hand that the capitalist
is an arrogant monopolistic oppressor, and on the
other hand it begets the feeling and idea among
employers that the laborers are ignorant, gullible
weaklings, led by the nose by a few idle and designing demagogues who seek only to stir up strife that
they may have an easy living, with prominence and
good pay.

It is peculiar that labor struggles are becoming
more and more struggles over the rights of unions and
recognition of unions than over strictly economic
propositions. The great Carnegie conflict, which constitutes such a sad page in the industrial history of
Pennsylvania, was largely a war on this point. The
great fight in Australia a few years ago was also a
real war, not over wages, but over recognition. In
writing of the leaders of the strike at the Broken Hill
Mines in Australia, the economist to whom I refer
quotes this description of the leaders who had been
sent to jail because of their part in the strike :

" The leaders, who are now serving sentences in jail,
showed themselves to be professional agitators pure
and simple. Possessed of the gift of fluent speech,
these men, not miners by calling at all, had foisted
themselves upon the workers' associations, and by the

rhetorical trick of inflaming envious passions and stir-
ring up strife between the employers and the employed,
had soon attained to positions of personal ascendency,
the toleration of which among large bodies of fairly-
educated, self-respecting workingmen is almost incredible. The strike was the very opportunity desired
by the leaders. At one bound they became persons
of public importance, issuing fierce manifestoes, having
their speeches telegraphed across a great continent,
visiting their pickets like generals in the field, being
huzzaed by the mob as they passed along the streets,
and generally living in a constant vapor-bath of self-
esteem and servile flattery. All these are simply the
necessary preliminaries to securing a seat in Parlia-
ment, and what to a man of the working classes is a
very large income, $300 per annum, with no real
hard work to do, with free railway traveling and invi-
tations to official dinners."

I refer to this simply to show the spirit in which
this movement is viewed. It is unquestionably true
that what the author says applies to some individual
cases in the labor movement.   It applies to quite as
large, and I think a very much larger, number in politics. There are more demagogues on the stump at
every election in the interest of regular political work
in any one state than the whole labor movement of the
United States together ever had at one time, or perhaps
in its whole history. This is the spirit of unfairness,
of hostility, not the spirit of understanding and recognizing the true inwardness of the case. It is this very
spirit which makes the demagogues. It is this very
spirit of hostility against organization *per se* that
makes the laborers cling together and follow the

demagogues, because they are at least on their side. We put up with everything in the face of the enemy, and to the extent that the employing class and the literary representatives of the employing class exhibit this spirit they make the laborers feel that the employers are their enemies.

This is all a mistake, as I have said a great many times ; and if I had the power I would write it on the sky, that no man should escape reading it, because it is fundamental. It has to do with the spirit of the great labor conflict, and, as I have said, the labor movement as a movement is inevitable in the nature of our present industrial society, and therefore it must of necessity be organized in order to be orderly, and if it must be organized and orderly then its organization and its organized representatives must be recognized ; recognized as respectable, recognized as legitimate delegates of their class, of their industry, just as much as the governor of a state is the representative of the people for the time being, though sometimes he is a fool and sometimes a demagogue and a humbug. The hope of getting a better governor is to appeal to the good sense of the people who elect him, and suggest a better one. The hope of getting better representatives among the labor organizations is, first, to get the confidence of the great mass of the laborers that we are not hostile to them and their organization as such, and then to encourage them to act through representatives, and point out that the more intelligent and capable their representatives the better will their interests be guarded, and the more frequently will they succeed in getting their rational demands conceded without the tumult and loss and disadvantages of strikes.

It should be a part of sound political doctrine then, to recognize this general condition, and by that I mean not so much that laws are needed, but that it should go without question that the rights of organized labor are to be recognized and treated with just as much as the individual rights of citizens; that this shall be a part of our political thinking, and that our legislatures, no matter of what party, and our governors or other executives, shall act upon this general assumption.

With this attitude once established the question is: What then ought the state to do? What can it do in the line of its legitimate, permanent functions? It is not my purpose here to name a specific platform, for that is an ever-varying thing; but it is rather to outline what I regard as the field of the state's action. There are certain kinds of things that the community can do and must do, in view of the fact that laborers have lost the right, by the very force of industrial evolution, to act individually. They must now be treated collectively, and there are a great many things that can be exacted collectively as well by the laborers through their organizations as they can by the state through political institutions. Here we come to the sort of objections that have become classic in the literature of political economy. The assumption is generally made, or at least too generally, in the spirit to which I have referred, that the individual is the only proper person to contract for all his industrial conditions. This is put forth as a conclusive reason against all industrial legislation directly affecting the laboring class.

Take the conspicuous case, for instance, of the hours of labor. The writer to whom I have referred lays

9

down this proposition as an axiom :—"Business prospers in the absence of legal interference, except to simply provide for justice and freedom." He gives as an illustration—and I quote this because it is typical of much of the respectable literature on the subject,—the case of the right of the laborer to be unhampered by legislation. Time, he says, is the laborer's capital, it is the one thing which the laborers have as much of as the rich.

Now, that is the very reason it is not capital. To say the poor have as much capital as the rich is to say something worse than silly. Capital is wealth, and any sort of hair-splitting and quibbling which calls a thing capital which the poor have as much of as the rich is mere talk without meaning. The poor have as much sunshine as the rich ; sometimes they have more than they need,—they are forced to stay in it too long. Shall we say then that the poor are as well off as the rich because, of the very indispensable requirements of life—air and sunshine,—they have as much? The occupant of the East Side tenement has as much time as Rockefeller. Here is a specimen of that kind of reasoning :—

"Time is the one thing that all share alike. Unlike nearly everything else, the poor have the same amount as the rich. It is, in fact, the capital of the laboring man. By Natural Law, he has his full time to dispose of as he may think best. But when he asks for an artificial law, which forcibly, under all circumstances, will deprive him of the use of a portion of his own productive power, as by an 'eight-hour law,' he diminishes by so much his available reserve and renders himself poorer. This is the real sum and substance of restrictive legislation regarding hours of labor, whenever applied to adults."

I would not quote this merely because it is in a book on *The Political Economy of Natural Law*, if it did not reflect so completely a general attitude and argument presented on the subject of the state's duty to labor. In Massachusetts, for instance, the most advanced state in the Union on that subject, the Arkwright Club, which is a club of New England manufacturers, has recently issued a pamphlet prepared by S. N. D. North, Secretary of the Wool Manufacturers' Association, especially to show the injury to labor of the shortening of the working day.

One would think that experience would count, but it seems not to count against a stereotyped habit of thinking. For nearly one hundred years the world has been experimenting on this very subject. It began in England in 1802. Ever since then all civilized countries, not excluding Russia, have done something in the direction of shortening the working day by legislative enactment, and in no case has the experiment diminished "by so much" the laborer's "available reserve," as the writer I have been quoting puts it, and rendered him poorer. In other words, in no instance has the laborer been poorer or in any way injured. On the contrary, the whole history of the subject is the history of an improvement in the laborer's condition, in his wages, in his social life and habits, in his intelligence, in his quality of citizenship and personal manhood. The assumption that time is the laborer's capital is mere sophistry.

As a matter of fact, the laborer has very little capital. The laborer has labor to sell, and the established rule, over which he has little control, by which that labor is sold is just the same rule as that by which hats, coats, iron, lead, leather or cloth are sold, *viz. :* on the basis of marginal cost, and the cost to the laborer is not the hours there are in each revolution of the earth, it is not the twenty-four hours at his disposal, but the cost is the social expense of his living. It makes no difference whether he has eight hours' service to sell each day or eighteen. If a group of laborers can live, without social ostracism, on twenty cents a day, then twenty cents a day is what they will command, and no more. If, through social education and opportunity and personal development, the social life which their surroundings demand cannot be supplied for less than two dollars a day, they will get two dollars, whether they have eight hours or eighteen. It is not true, in short, and never was, that a man's wages increase in proportion to the number of hours' labor he can sell each day. On the contrary, they often increase as the hours diminish ; not because they diminish, however, but because he is a more valuable social unit.

Now, the duty of the state is to contribute everything which well help make the laborer a more valuable social factor in the community. Whatever contributes to that is for the public welfare, as well as for the welfare of the individual laborer himself. The state is interested in producing a high type of citizenship, because a high type of citizenship gives the best security to all institutions of society. It gives the highest type of civilized culture, and the least possible need of repressive institutions. The state, I repeat, is interested in producing a high type of manhood. Whatever will contribute to that will contribute to the welfare of all classes in the community.

There are many things that the laborers can do to promote this. They can organize. They can demand from their employers and from the community many things by voluntary effort, by organized demand. There are many things, however, that they cannot do, neither individually nor in their voluntary organizations, as well as the state can do these things for them. It is these particular things, or this class of things, that it is the state's duty to furnish. They are always in the line of, as I have said, *opportunity*. The instance just referred to, of shortening the hours of labor, is one of the most conspicuous of this kind. Why? Why should the state care about how long the laborers work? Because that has a great deal to do with the possible social life of the laborers, and thus it has a great deal to do with their opportunities for education, for culture, for individual expansion; in a word, with their possibilities of social improvement. The conditions under which laborers work, the sanitary conditions, the protection of machinery, are of great social as well as health protective importance. To see that these conditions are wholesome, cheerful, encouraging, is a part of the protective function of the public. It cannot always be demanded by the laborers themselves; they cannot always reach this through their organizations. Then how can it and should it be reached? Through their action at the ballot box.

There are many reasons why this is a legitimate part of the duty or function of the state with regard to labor. In the first place, employers are not, in the nature of things, likely to see these necessities. They come in their way. The things that they see are the economies, the conditions that make for profits, and for successful conducting of the business. That which affects the mere personality of the laborers, the social conveniences, the psychological influences surrounding laborers, is least likely to impress the employers. These things are observed more frequently by people who have better and higher ideas of life and possible social conditions. To the employers, at first, all such changes, like shortening the hours of labor, boxing of machinery, furnishing fire-escapes and adding expensive appointments to the workshop, all mean increased outlay, and this increases, at least for the time, the cost of production. If one manufacturer, as the result of a strike, is forced, for instance, to make a large outlay for things which do not immediately contribute to an increased product, it has the effect of temporarily putting him at a disadvantage in competing with his neighbors who are getting along without these outlays.

That is the first circumstance which brings resistance on the part of the employer. But when the state says: " You shall have fire-escapes at every window or on every floor, you shall have certain methods of ventilation, even though it involves a great cost, you shall have all machinery guarded, no matter if it costs ten per cent. more," and so on, it says it to them all. It says, these are the conditions under which this industry shall be conducted. That puts no one employer to a disadvantage with his competitors. If every manufacturing concern, for instance, is restricted to eight or nine instead of ten or eleven or twelve hours a day, no one manufacturer is at a disadvantage on that account. If every corporation is compelled to spend ten or

twenty thousand dollars for improvements and conveniences in the workshops, it is at no special disadvantage because all its competitors have to do the
same. This is not interfering with the freedom of industry. It is not affecting the opportunities of the
employer. It is simply determining the plane on
which business shall be conducted and competition take
place. It simply says: " On this civilized plane only
shall this class of business be conducted in this community." This includes, too, all the protective legislation of the factory acts, employers' liability acts, *etc.*,
which have been developed to perfection in England
and ought to be enacted in every state in this country
where factory methods prevail.

The same principle comes right into our city life.
Take the sweatshop, for instance. There we have a
system of employment which is at once undermining the
health and stultifying the social life of the workers,
besides creating a repressing influence on all legitimate workshop production. The theory that every
individual has a right to dispose of his own labor in
his own way, and make whatever use of his time and
under whatever conditions he pleases, provided he does
not interfere with the rights of other people, is capable
of a great deal of sophistical application. It is used
in defense of the sweatshop system. This system con-
verts the homes of our laborers into workshops, and
somebody says : Who has the right to interfere and
say what a man shall do in his own home ? Long ago
civilization decided that the state has the right to interfere with what shall be done anywhere and everywhere. The state already says that certain kinds of
plumbing and ventilation shall exist in every city home.

Why should not a person be permitted to live without ventilation and plumbing in his house, and without any modern sanitary appointments at all, if he chooses? The answer is, because it is inimical to the welfare of society, and no one individual, because of his low desires or meager wants or traditional barbarism, can be permitted to live under conditions which jeopardize directly or indirectly the health and well-being of other members of the community. There are hundreds of families who would be perfectly willing if they had the smallpox to go right on sending other members of their family to school or to the workshop, or visit their neighbors and have their neighbors visit them, and they growl because necessity says they shall be quarantined. But the point is now reached at which everybody demands that quarantine shall be enforced. What does that mean? It means that the liberty of these poeple shall stop short at that point; that the highest civilization guarantees the greatest freedom for all, and in guaranteeing that liberty it restricts the liberty of anybody to do that which shall interfere with the welfare of all.

The sweatshop is clearly a case of social injury. The conditions under which manufacture is conducted in these dens, as I have said, are detrimental to the health as well as depressing to the social condition of the entire class. As a matter of public policy it is the duty of the state to interfere in behalf of the laboring class. Why? Because the laborers cannot interfere for themselves. The laborers cannot make a personal appeal to these ignorant Poles who huddle in tenement houses and live and work and eat and sleep on the benches with their tailoring. They cannot enforce a reform because they have no legal right to enforce industrial and social conditions upon others. It is the state only that can intervene, and it is clearly the state's duty to do so.

This is a part of the protective function of the state, the same as it is a part of the duty of the state to enforce educational conditions upon the children of the community. Why should the state insist upon education? Because education is a part of the preparation for good citizenship, and individual initiative is not strong enough, voluntary organization is not adequate to give it; the state alone is the power which can enforce this educational and therefore protective influence.

The relation of the state to labor, then, is not only very important but it is not unclear or difficult to understand, if we will recognize a few fundamental facts regarding it. First, that much can be done by laborers to improve their condition by voluntary association, and it is the duty, therefore, of the public and of the state to recognize the legitimacy of that association. Second, that there are a large number of things which the laborers cannot do individually, because of their changed industrial condition; and which they cannot do by voluntary association because of their limited influence and lack of authority; and which, therefore, must be done by the state. These needs are constantly arising. They cannot be particularized at any given time as permanently including the whole docket. They are constantly arising as new conditions are created, but the general duty is very clear, and it is that the state should constantly exercise its influence and authority in determining the conditions under which industries shall be conducted, contracts be made, and laborers, as well as everybody else, live.

This is a wide field to cover, though the principle of action is simple. It is a wide field because the experiences are constantly increasing and interests constantly multiplying in which the capitalist employer, in the effort to compete and develop new methods and get the maximum product, tends to ignore the need of improvements in the industrial or labor side of these new conditions. It is therefore of paramount importance to the public policy of the country that this rational and permanent relation of the state to labor be recognized as a part of our political system and as a part of the necessary function of government; so that it shall not be opposed on abstract principle, as economists and employers are in the habit of doing, but that the question shall ever be, will it produce the effect desired? Is the reform a needed one? Is it along the line of guarding the opportunities for and possibilities of gradual self-improvement for the laborers? If it is, no considerations of individual capital should stand in the way, and if we always make the conditions general, as the state must, capital is not injured by the action, because, as I have said before, whatever affects everybody is not a relative disadvantage to anybody. That is why it is important that so many of these reforms, which are perfectly feasible, perfectly rational, and indispensable to the progress of society, must be made by the state, because the state alone can make them general, and it is their general application that eliminates all individual disadvantage.

If this policy were intelligently recognized and adopted it would do more than almost anything else to eliminate the irregularity and unreason from the often impetuous demands of labor. When the legitimacy of the principle is recognized, discussion of the details can proceed with reason and sense. Knowledge of the case must then be insisted upon for the representatives of labor, and this will make necessary more intelligent leaders on the labor side. When it is a recognized fact that the state has a legitimate function in relation to labor; that the principle of these demands is not denied, but that it is only a question of the facts in the case, then there is no longer any excuse on the part of the laborers to cry "enemy" at every capitalist, and there is less room for demagogues to inflame the masses with charges of capitalistic hostility. The laborers then would find that their cause rested not upon mere antagonism to capital, but upon proving the merits of the case, and this would send home each time the necessity of intelligent conception and ununderstanding of their own condition. They would learn from time to time that their cause was lost by the ignorance or incapacity of their representatives, and not by any general antagonism of the legislatures or the community on the subject. Thus, competency instead of demagogy would become the required quality in labor representatives, and this would tend rapidly to lift the discussion of labor problems from the plane of physical combat to that of intelligent, economic controversy.

X.

THE ERA OF TRUSTS *

It is manifest, even to casual observers, that we are entering upon an industrial era of trusts. Within a year, and especially during the last six months, the tendency towards reorganization and consolidation of a number of smaller industries into large ones has amounted almost to a stampede. Nothing like it was ever known before since the origin of the factory system. If this movement continues during the present year at anything like the rate it has been going the last six months, the leading industries of this country will have taken on the trust form of organization. Whether this movement will be permanent or will arouse public opposition which will bring its defeat through legislative restriction, will depend almost entirely upon the wisdom of the capitalists themselves.

The movement itself is an entirely natural one and is wholly in line with economic progress, provided it is not uneconomically directed. If these re-organizations are conducted on sound business principles, as in the adoption of new machinery, *viz.:* to create profits by the introduction of economies in administration and sharing these profits with the community through a reasonable lowering of prices, there will be no serious

---

¹ Published in *Gunton's Magazine* of March, 1899.

danger of political molestation. But if the re-organiz-
ation becomes a speculative game to take advantage of
an industrial sentiment for the purpose of monopolizing
certain lines of industry and "gouging" the public by
putting up prices, to pay dividends on abnormal capi-
talization for promoters' bonuses, a social opposition
which will take on a political form is pretty certain to
arise.   There is already an antagonism to trusts, from
sheer economic prejudice, largely born of socialistic antagonism to capital and partly stimulated by popular
aversion to the new ; but, on the whole, thus far trusts
have been fairly economic in their policy.   In a few instances they have departed from business principles and
tried to establish uneconomic monopolies, and in every
such instance they have come to grief.   But this unwholesome effort has created an unfavorable impression
in the public mind.   All the trusts and large concentrations which have become permanently established have
contributed very largely to the improvement of the
products they furnish, and greatly reduced the price.

It is characteristic of all these large concerns, which
have followed sound business principles and shared their
profits with the public by reducing the cost of the product, that they are in the long run the most successful
establishments.   Moreover, these concerns are rapidly
outgrowing public antagonism. But, on the other hand,
a number of the industries now going through the
process of reorganization are following the speculative,
monopolistic, rather than the economic method of procedure.   They are using the concentration of the industry as a means not only to lessen the expense of production but also to put up the price of the product to
the community. Now, this is not merely uneconomic

but it is against the public welfare and will not long be tolerated—and it should not. The result of this policy, if it is pursued, will be to array the public through the legislatures against the trust movement altogether, and thus work great injury to the community in general.

With the return of prosperity the universal impulse is again to make profits. Confidence has everywhere been revived. The demand for goods is rapidly increasing. New investments to supply anticipated demands are being freely made. In short, all the signs point to another era of prosperity. But the people have become accustomed to the low prices established during the era of depression, and it is more than probable that any attempt to reestablish former profits by reinaugurating former prices would greatly check, if it did not destroy, the present business boom. Profits once lost by falling prices, except under the sudden pressure of war or depreciated currency, can never be permanently reestablished by raising prices, but must necessarily come through new profit-creating methods, either in the form of improved machinery or more economic type of organization. Though not much understood, this fact is universally felt throughout the industrial world.

It is true throughout society that every class or group has to suffer for the sins of its most injudicious or hot-headed members. Trade unionists as a class labor under suspicion and distrust, and encounter considerable open opposition, because of the foolish and ignorant acts of a few hot-headed leaders who become conspicuous at the moment of a strike. So it is with capitalists. A few mean, unreasoning, and perhaps unthinking capitalists, who are only up to the level of making business a grand game of grab, bring discredit in the popular mind upon the whole employing class. Laborers and their sympathizers in the community follow the same rule that employers do toward labor unions, and judge the whole class by their worst specimens.

This is true of the public's attitude towards all new movements, and the present trust movement will be no exception. If a few concerns are unfortunate enough to be under a leadership sufficiently short-sighted to take advantage of the temporary opportunity the new organization affords to tax the public by increased prices, there is sure to be a vigorous crusade against the new movement. It will not be confined to the few indiscreet concerns that have not learned to recognize the highest business success, but it will be directed against capital and large organizations in general.

The tin-plate trust is one of these offensive examples.[1] This is an industry which practically could not have existed in this country but for the legislative aid of the public. Until the tariff—a very high one at first —was placed upon foreign tin, the tin-plate industry had no existence in the United States. It has been born and nurtured by the protective aid the public has given it. Its very existence is due to the good will and political good sense of the United States. The tin-plate trust is one of the "fool examples" of using the trust organization to put up the price. Of course it would be unwise for the public to hamper a really helpful industrial movement because speculative " grab-

---

[1] In this connection see Chapter XII., " The Tin-Plate Trust."

bers " get temporary possession ; nor should a few mistakes of this kind be permitted to be used effectively against the protective tariff as a general policy. Nevertheless it would be perfectly safe and the part of good policy for congress to pass a law empowering and instructing the secretary of the treasury to withdraw the protective duty from all products the prices of which are raised by trust organizations. In short, the moment a trust organization raises the price of a product enjoying any degree of protective duty, it should thenceforth be put upon the free list and become subject at once to world competition. If the organizers of trusts in any line have not economic sense and public spirit enough to refrain from using their concentrated power to tax the public by increasing prices, the public should at once withdraw any protective advantage it has given to that industry. The primary object of protection is to make it possible to stimulate the development of domestic industries ; but when industries have become established and proceed to take advantage of this protection for monopolistic, price-raising purposes, they should at once be thrown on their own competitive resources. This would be in harmony with strictly economic policy, and might have a wholesome effect upon the movement of trust reorganization.

We should utilize the coming period of prosperity to give to capital liberal profits, to laborers higher wages, and to the public better and cheaper goods. If the benefits of the trust era are thus distributed it will be an era of permanent advance in public welfare and social harmony as well as in economic organization.

XI.

MACHINERY AND LABOR DISPLACEMENT *

IN taking up the question of machinery and labor displacement, I want to discuss it with entire frankness, and as fully as the time will permit. In the first place we might as well recognize the painful fact that the ignorance on this subject is not all on the side of the laborers. The capitalists in the main do not display more information and general familiarity with this topic than do the laborers. The capitalists know that finally, under pressure of competition, to join larger organizations is their only salvation. They know that this is beneficial to them, because it saves their life, industrially ; and therefore they think that everybody who does not know that is to be designated with a very short name. On the other hand, the laborers know something. They know that in this struggle they come up against a great many unforeseen hardships. They know that it is necessary for them very frequently to organize, and through their organizations do a great many things that seem very irrational to the community, and they conclude that if the employers cannot see the wisdom of this they must be very ignorant and are equally entitled to be dismissed with a short name. The fact is, and it is a painful one but very vital, that

---

* Lecture delivered in New York City, April 18th, 1899.

neither party seems to understand the position of the other, nor their relation to the general situation.

The question that I want to consider is the increasing organization tendency of capital and the actual effect upon the community, including the laborers and consumers, of this labor-displacing and industry re-adjusting movement.

First of all, let us inquire for a minute or two into the actual relation of capital and labor to the community. Capital must be definitely recognized as capital. It is not a person. It has neither flesh nor blood, soul nor conscience. It is a thing. It is capital, to be used by the capitalist. The public interest in the use of this tool—capital—is not in its ownership but in its products.

Labor is not a tool. Labor is the service of individuals, and represents the great mass of the community. Therefore labor and laborers cannot be considered under any circumstances as the equivalent of tools. In labor is embodied the conditions of civilization. Therefore, while capital as a tool should be secured as cheaply as possible, and used as long as possible, and thrown away as soon as it ceases to be economic, labor cannot be so treated. Labor must be treated in the productive process not as an instrument but as a social factor. The community, which includes capitalists, laborers and all other elements, has also a stake in this movement.

It is quite clear that neither labor nor capital will put forth its best effort and serve the community at its maximum efficiency without a stimulating reward. The reward of the capitalist is profit—an increased increment of wealth. The reward of laborers as laborers is wages. The interest of the community in the general result (which includes, as I have said, capitalists and laborers and all other social units) is in the quality and price of the products. So there we have the three forms in which the benefits, if any, accruing from capitalistic production are distributed to the community ; profits, wages, and diminishing prices. The capitalists and laborers, therefore, each have two forms of partaking in the results of this movement ; capitalists in profits, and in declining prices to the extent of their own consumption ; laborers in wages and declining prices, and the rest of the community only in the declining prices or cheapening of wealth.

It is commonly assumed both by capitalists and laborers that they should have all the gain there is from the application of new methods to productive enterprises. The capitalist pays for the new machine, perhaps pays a royalty to the inventor ; and, with his narrow view, thinks that all the advantage accruing from that machine therefore belongs to him. If the machine will produce twice as much for the same investment as could be produced before, he thinks that is the equitable reward for his ingenuity in knowing enough to buy the new machine.

The laborer, on the other hand, who works the machine and finds that it will produce twice as much in an hour as the old machine that he used, imagines that he is the one entitled to all this increased product. He says—not theoretically but actually—: " I produced twice as much to-day as I did ten or twenty years ago, or as my father did working at the same industry, and I only get ten per cent. more in wages. I am robbed of the other ninety per cent. which I produce." This is not merely in the abstract ; it is the concrete statement that

goes the round and has been going the round for fifty
years,—in fact, ever since machinery began to be introduced.   A few years ago the cotton operatives of Lancashire sent a deputation to London to interview a parliamentary committee upon this subject, and they pointed
out that their product had been increased several hun-
dred-fold while their wages had risen only about fifty
per cent.,—and even so able a statistician as Mr. Giffen,
then president of the British Statistical Society, admitted the gist if not the extent of their complaint,
and said :—"It may be admitted, to begin with, that
there is apparent foundation for some of the complaints.   Workmen in particular industries do not get
a reward at all in proportion to the increase of production in those employments.   The illustration of a cotton
mill is familiar.   A single attendant on a number of
machines will ' produce' as much in an hour as formerly in a year or two, but his wages are only double—
or perhaps not quite double—what they were when he
produced so much less."

When a statistician and economist like Mr. Giffen
admits this, it is not surprising that the laborers should
insist upon it as a matter of fact.   However, this is
not merely an unjust and unreasonable complaint, but
what the laborers expect in this particular is absolutely
impossible.   Economically it cannot be, and morally
it ought not to be.   So long as it is insisted that the
laborer who uses the new machine is entitled to all the
increased product of the machine; or, on the other
hand, so long as the capitalist imagines that because
he bought the new machine he is entitled to all the
increased product of it, there never can be any rational
attitude on this subject.   As a matter of fact, both of

these claims, as I said, are economically and morally erroneous.

In the first place, what has the capitalist done to cause this immense increase of production by this new machine? He simply invested the money in it when it became clear that the investment would yield a larger return than an investment in any other line he knew about. He did nothing to bring the invention into existence or to create the social conditions that made its utility possible. He acted upon it wholly and absolutely as an investment.

On the other hand, what did the laborer do? Just nothing at all. He did not even make the investment. The chief thing he did was to resist its introduction, make it seem to be as inefficient as possible, and for a long time declare that it was no good, that it would not do the work, even spoiling the work deliberately in order to discredit the new machine. The laborer may be said absolutely to contribute nothing at all to the new process, but rather to act consciously as an impediment to its success. Why should either one of these two, then, run away with all the advantage? Certainly they should not.

What relation has the community to the matter? The community—and both capitalist and laborer are included in this—furnishes the great background for making this improvement possible. Civilization, with its growing and diversified demands, furnishes the increased consumption, the market, which makes a greater aggregate production profitable. This is the great social fact which society in its aggregate furnishes, and it constitutes at once the opportunity and the incentive for the new machinery or new organization which creates the larger output. Therefore the community has a greater claim, and in fact the greatest claim, upon the fruits of this improvement. The capitalist, of course, will have, in his special form of profits, a part of this gain. This he gets by investing in the new instrument before all his competitors have got it. The laborers as laborers have no special claim upon it other than the claim their social standard gives them for higher wages, but as a part of the whole community they have a claim upon it in the form of reduced prices.

Now, if the capitalist should take it all in profits, or the laborers who work these particular machines should take it all in increased wages, or even if the particular capitalists and laborers (say in the cotton factories or shoe factories) should take all the advantage of these machines, then the community which had really made it possible—all the other capitalists and laborers and all others—would get none of the advantages. That would be neither good economics nor good ethics. The mason and the bricklayer, the architect and the builder, the painter and designer, all are as much entitled to the benefits of an invention in the production of shoes or of cotton cloth as the people who happen to work the machines which create the economy. If this were not so, then that great class in the community, including most of the agriculturists and all the industries where new machinery is not adopted, would get none of the benefits of the great productive improvements due to the advance of society. If this were possible, progress itself would be arrested; because if they could get none of the advantages of the application of science to production they would not and could

not become a part of the great increased consuming force
of the community.   If the bricklayers and agricultural
laborers and those who work in non-machine-using
industries could not participate in the increased consumption of machine products the market would be so
small that the improved machines could not be used.
If nobody used cotton cloth but those who made it, it
would have to be made by hand, as it was in India
hundreds of years ago.   The fact that society in its
aggregate develops the intelligence and inventive impulse, and second that it also furnishes the consuming
capacity or market demand, are the two great facts
that make the use of machinery possible ; and thus it
is obvious that the products of industrial improvements
should be distributed throughout the community.
They should not, and cannot without injury to the
community, be monopolized either by the particular
capitalist or the particular laborers who use the improved methods.

Clearly, then, the laborer who makes twenty times
as many shoes in a day as his grandfather did, and the
weaver who weaves five hundred times as many yards
of cloth as his grandfather did at the hand loom, cannot and ought not to get five hundred times as much.
His rise of wages represents his direct demand upon
the sources of production, as reflected in his increased
standard of living.   The increased profits, which are
only temporary, are the special reward of the capitalist
for his investment in the new machine ; but, in the
nature of economic law, the tendency of this increased
production due to the new machines is to set the employers competing one with another for the market
demand for these goods, and in this competition the

price is lowered. By this lowering of the price the whole community shares the advantage. That part of the improvement which goes to increase profits stays with the capitalist only so long as he can keep his lead; that part which goes to increase wages stays with the laborer, and he keeps it forever; and that part which comes in reduced prices comes to the bricklayer and carpenter and printer and agriculturist and, in short, to the entire community, and so the benefits of progress in this direction are distributed throughout society. That is, in fact, the most equitable adjustment of the matter.

I mention this simply to call attention to the unreasonableness and injustice, as well as uneconomic character, of the demand that all of this gain belongs to the particular people who happen to use the new instruments. In truth, the benefit belongs to all the influences which produced the new instrument, and the chief of these is society in its market capacity. Where society is simple and non-expensive, as in China, this new increment does not arise. The capitalist will not invest his money in a new invention. Why? Because he cannot sell its product. If he does invest he will lose by it. Society furnishes him no market background, no demand for the results, and consequently his profits do not come. The reason is not that the laborers are not so willing, or that the capitalists are not so willing, in China as in England or the United States, to increase their output; but it is the fact that society in its aggregate demand does not furnish the opportunity and incentive.

It is this fact, that the greater part of the increased product of civilization goes to the public in lower prices rather than in permanently increased profits or very high wages in special industries, that constitutes the great equitable element in economic distribution.   As I said, the capitalist gets his large profit at first, in proportion as he anticipates his competitors in introducing the improved instrument; but as fast as his competitors adopt the same methods he has to surrender his great profits to the community in the lower prices and create a new margin by another improvement.   So that, the profits of the capitalist from any given improvement are temporary.   They are large at first, but necessarily tend to diminish through competition until they reach the vanishing point.   Almost every industry where much machinery is employed has gone through this process several times during the last half century.   In the various departments of iron and steel manufacture, and of furniture and clothing, this cycle has been traversed several times.   In the production of cotton cloth the cycle has been traversed probably some five or six times since 1830.   The high-profit man who was using the best machinery in 1830 became the low-profit man before 1845, and so on in each round of competition until the cotton cloth that was sold in 1830 at seventeen cents a yard is now sold for about three or four cents a yard or less.   That difference between seventeen cents and four cents has been given to the public in lower prices.   The aggregate profit in 1830 was not greater than—perhaps not so great as—in 1899, but the new machines one after another have created new margins of profits, and as soon as each new machine came into general use the profit disappeared and passed to the public.   In that way it occurs in all progressive society that profits from new

machines are not permanent but temporary, and their
duration depends on the rate of the progress of improvement. In some industries the profits last only a
few years, when a new invention comes along and
transfers them to the public.

On the wage side, however, the process of gain is
permanent. While increased profits are temporary, increased wages are everlasting. Wages recede only with
the collapse of society, because higher wages come not
by the temporary advantage of a new instrument but
by the permanent elevation of the social standard of
the laborers. So that, every addition to wages—I
mean every general addition—is a permanent addition
to the welfare of the wage class. Strikes, and even
revolution and political disruption, will set in before
wages can be permanently pushed back very far.
Indeed, this republic could not stand if by any process
wages should be put back to the standard of 1830 or
1840. But the income of capital can be pushed back
two or three times in a decade if new improvements
in production are constantly introduced. The capitalists realize a part of this general trend, and the
laborers realize another part, but neither seem fully
to realize the general trend for both.

As I have said a great many times, the movement of
advancing wages, lowering prices, and shortening
hours of labor, is the movement of civilization. There
can be no real progress without it. On the other
hand, it is equally true that this movement in wages
and prices by which the laborers get the only advantage they ever get, and the community gets its share
of progress, is impossible unless capitalistic economy
in the process of production also takes place. While

it is true to a large extent that rising wages are the cause of lowering prices, in that the increased wages lead to increased expenditures which in turn furnish the market basis for the use of better methods and larger production, yet the increased wages and lowering prices cannot come permanently without being accompanied by improved methods of production in some direction. This is the point where the working-men, and the public for that matter, are confused.

This improvement in the process of production comes in two ways; one by more perfect organization, the other by more perfect machines. It is a peculiar feature in the history of industrial progress that both these movements have always met with popular opposition. From time immemorial every effort to introduce a capitalistic economy in production, either by better organization (which means larger concerns) or better machinery, has always been regarded by the laborers, and usually by the public, as hostile to popular welfare. Even Mill once went so far as to say: "It is doubtful if improved machinery has lightened the toil of a single laborer." This feeling, which among the laborers becomes a conviction, is so general that it forms a popular belief, almost universally accepted and relied upon. It may really be called an economic superstition.

There is reason for this, or it could not exist. The reason is, of course, that the immediate effect of all new inventions is some displacement. For instance, improved organization—and by improved of course I mean more economic organization, of the kind that saves waste or accomplishes a great deal more with less effort,—must necessarily, in order to be worth while, do the same or more work with fewer people. The very fact that this occurs involves some displacement. The large concerns displace some of the smaller shops; that is to say, small shops which wasted a great deal of energy and expense in doing very little, and consequently charged the public a higher price.

When a larger concern does the same work more efficiently and less expensively, the small concern necessarily is compelled to do one of two things—either reorganize itself and become a part of a larger concern, or else leave the business.

It is this displacement which creates the friction. The person who is displaced thinks the whole world is being displaced the same as he is. Moreover, he thinks that the displacement is a permanent misfortune, seeing only just what affects himself personally; and he raises a cry against the movement which is doing the displacing. The general idea that capital is selfish and grasping and that the weak man is the victim lends itself to the sentiment that this displacement is working an injury to society.

What takes place with reference to displacement of small concerns takes place in the case of laborers by the introduction of new machines. The new machine must displace or it can never accomplish any economy, it cannot create a larger profit, it cannot furnish lower prices, and it cannot yield higher wages or shorter hours. It is the very displacement that is the test of the efficiency or the degree of economy which a new device will introduce. Is this displacement permanent; is it a permanent evil, or is it only temporary? It is quite clear that the workingmen have always believed—and there are many others who

share this belief—that the evil is permanent; that it
is a real affliction upon the laboring class and consequently upon the community, introduced by capital
for its own selfish ends.   The history of industrial
advance is also the history of resistance to innovations.   When the first inventions of the factory system were introduced, before the middle of the eighteenth century, Crompton and Hargreaves and Arkwright were mobbed by their fellow hand-workers for
having introduced the machines.   In 1779 mobs
marched from town to town in England and broke
the new machines, and still later they did the same by
the power loom.   The ruins of some of the old factories in which the power looms were broken and
other machinery demolished still remain in England
as a monument to this opposition to the first introduction of steam-driven machinery.   There has probably
never been a really efficient labor-saving machine
introduced since the power loom which has not met
with this opposition.

The trade unions, which are the great stronghold
and social weapon of the laboring class, practically
make it a part of their creed to oppose the introduction of new machines.   Many have been the strikes
against the introduction of new machines into the
workshop.   The opposition of the laborers has not
been because they disliked the new machine but because they saw that it discharged some laborers and
believed that it permanently displaced them, so as to
increase the ranks of enforced idleness.   They see the
local fact, which is temporary, and they treat it as a
general and permanent fact.   They see the laborer
discharged, and they do not see any power associated

with the cause which discharged him that tends to furnish him another job.

It is not to be denied that the new machine discharges labor, displaces a portion of the employed force, or else enlarges the production with the same labor force, which is economically the same thing. It would not be labor-saving if it did not do that. But if it did only that it would not be a permanent benefit. If the laborers were correct in the belief that the introduction of labor-saving machines permanently increases enforced idleness, they would be entirely right in regarding new machinery as detrimental to the laborer's interest. But, is it not easy to see that if new machines contributed directly to the aggregate of permanent enforced idleness in proportion as they created economy in the cost of production, the consuming power of the community would diminish directly as improved machinery is used? The idler cannot buy, and this would be practically a diminution of the consumption directly as it increased the economy. In other words, it would be a means of producing more but of directly destroying the power to consume. If this were true, it is obvious that the market would begin to diminish as soon as the production increased, which would soon destroy the value of all the new machines by introducing an industrial depression and glutted market.

So that, the machines would not be a permanent benefit; prices could not be economically lowered, and wages could not rise. None of our industrial progress could have taken place if improved machinery meant permanent increase of idleness. In order to make this point clear, however, it is necessary to look at the concrete facts. General inferences are too vague for the man who is discharged, and this is becoming more and more an important question in society. For example, in the mercantile world, small shopkeepers are laboring under exactly this same superstition regarding larger concerns, especially department stores ; in manufacture, the small manufacturers are oppressed with this superstition regarding large corporations and trusts; and in all the lines of progressive industry where machinery is used the laborers are suffering from the same misapprehension.

At this time this subject has a special bearing on the condition of New England. New England was the first seat of the cotton industry in this country. It developed, first, small water wheels, then larger cotton factories with modern methods, and ultimately all the processes to which I have referred that have lowered the price of cotton cloth from seventeen to three cents a yard. Now a migration of the industry has set in, and the manufacture of coarser cotton goods (and ultimately the finer will follow suit) is going South. There is nothing unnatural in this. It is the migration of an industry towards its most natural point. Modern cotton manufacture did not begin in New England. It began in old England, in Lancashire, the farthest removed from any source of raw material. It began in England because England was the most advanced in industrial civilization. The inventions of the factory system took place in Lancashire. Consequently, cotton manufacture had its first half century of development in England. It then began to migrate from old England to New England. With the political encouragement which the pro-

tective tariff gave, still higher types of machinery and
forms of organization were developed in New England. Prices were lowered, wages were increased,
and hours of labor shortened; and, lastly, the industry
is now rapidly migrating from New England to the
southern states,—another transition. This makes the
problem a very very important one for the eastern
states. In the new mills in the South, largely built by
northern capital, the best machinery and appointments
are introduced. Wages are very much lower, hours of
labor are very much longer, and consequently severe
competition between New England and the southern
states has arisen. Those who can sell, quality being
the same, at the lowest price will have the business,
and the New England manufacturers found themselves with a higher cost of production than in the
South. They did as capitalists always do, tried to
overcome the difficulty at the point of least resistance,—which was to lower wages. Temporarily they
succeeded in doing that, but the forces of civilization
are ever constant, and with the return of prosperity in
the nation the laborers' standard of living reasserted
itself, and through their organizations they demand a
return of their former pay. This, a few weeks ago,
was granted. There was some talk among the employers that they were handicapped by the short-hour
legislation of Massachusetts and the other New England states, but civilization has written its word on
that subject. It is as impossible permanently to lower
wages and return to the eleven or twelve hour system
as it would be to brush back the tides of the ocean.
Progress has accomplished these things. The manufacturers of New England cannot hold their compet-

itive position by turning back the dial of progress. That they cannot and should not do,—better retire from business. But to retire from business would be to inflict catastrophe upon a great section of the American people. The sudden collapse of the cotton industry in New England would be a calamity to civilization.

There is only one way in which this calamity can be avoided ; the same way that previous readjustments have been accomplished, by the introduction of superior methods. The science and skill of the more advanced civilization must be the means of its defense against the new and less developed. The South cannot be beaten by a return to barbarism. When it comes to barbarism the South can win. The East, like all civilization, must protect itself industrially by rising to still higher productive methods.

As is usually the case when all other methods fail, capital is turning to this mode of relief. It being impossible permanently to reduce wages or to lengthen working hours, an appeal to inventive genius has been made and certain radically improved machines which have been in process of development for several years, particularly in the weaving department, have at last been completed. A new loom, manufactured by the Drapers, of Hopedale, Mass., is being introduced. This is an immense labor-saving device in the art of weaving. The advantage of it is that one weaver can mind more than double the number of looms that he can by the old method,—eight looms being the maximum at present, while with the new system twenty looms can be minded by a single weaver, as I saw a week ago.

Here the manufacturers are making a virtue of

necessity and doing what science, progress, and self-preservation for themselves and for the New England cotton manufacturing community for some time to come has made necessary. The operatives, through their unions, oppose and practically refuse to use the new looms, or to mind more of the new looms than they did of the old. Of course, if the weaver refuses to mind more than eight looms, then there is not a saving but a loss by introducing them, because they cost very much more than the old ones. If the laborers persist in this, they of course will succeed in doing one of two things, either stop the improvement and therefore prevent the development of the only method New England has of successfully competing with the South, thus permanently forcing New England into the position of a defeated industry, or else—what is even worse—force the introduction of an inferior population that will work for less wages and use the new looms too.

The reason assigned for this opposition is that it will discharge the weavers, that it will lead to displacement of a large portion of the operatives;—the same motive that caused resistance to the first power loom, to the printing press, the type-setting machine, and in fact to new machinery in every department of manufacture. Of course, they believe that this displacement will be permanent. Although this opposition has been presented to every innovation of the kind and has been shown by experience to be erroneous, yet it still asserts itself.

At first it would seem the height of stupidity, and yet, if we turn to the employers, who ought to be more intelligent, we find they act exactly the same on certain subjects; for instance, the hours of labor. From the time of the introduction of the first law in England to shorten the hours of labor, in 1802, to the very last in Massachusetts, in 1894, to reduce the hours to fifty-eight a week, the employers have repeated without variation, just as a parrot calls off the sound it has learned to make, the prediction that if the working day were shortened wages would be lowered; and yet in not a single instance has that ever occurred. On the contrary, either because of it or in spite of it, wages have risen as the hours of labor have diminished. This is the unbroken record of nearly a hundred years, and yet in the South, where they are asking only for a ten-hour law (which the English operatives got in 1847) the professors of political economy and the eloquent portrayers of history repeat the statement that this means a reduction of the wages of the laborers.

If we could trace the history of every manufacturing industry where machinery is used it would be easy to see that in nearly every case, and I know of no exceptions, where labor-saving machinery has been introduced, while it did cause a displacement, that displacement was always a re-arrangement and not a permanent discharge. On the contrary, with the re-arrangement there always has come a large increase in the number of laborers employed in that industry. Instead of permanently diminishing the number of laborers it has always increased the number of employees in that industry, and concurrently given rise to a number of new industries.

Take for instance the printing press, as represented in the almost automatic modern Hoe press, by which nearly all our great daily newspapers are now printed; the machine that takes a roll of paper and sends it flying through the rollers, printing it on both sides, cutting it off in proper lengths, folding it in sheets and putting in the supplements, and delivering at the other end ready for the news carrier,—a huge mechanism that seems almost to have human intelligence and is more than human in its accuracy. This has so reduced the cost of printing that one press to-day will print more papers than five thousand pressmen could print on the primitive single press, and yet, strange to say, there are more printers than ever before. Why? Because this press, together with type-setting machines, has so reduced the cost of printing that the daily paper can be sold for a penny and books can be sold for ten cents, giving them enormous circulations. The market for all printed matter has been so widened that there are not only several times more printers but the number employed in the manufacture of paper, in binding, and in the various tributary industries connected with the building of presses and the equipping of printing offices has doubled and trebled. It has, as I said, both increased the employment for printers and created several new tributary industries in which highly skilled and well-paid labor is employed.

If we could go through manufacturing industries in general we would find a similar experience in nearly all cases. The facts in the following table are taken from the United States Census of 1890. It shows the number of laborers employed in sixty-four industries in 1880 and 1890, and the annual wages in those years. The last two columns show the amount and per cent. of increase in wages.

INDUSTRY	NUMBER OF EMPLOYEES		YEARLY WAGES		AMOUNT OF INCREASE	PER CENT. OF AGE
	1880	1890	1880	1890		
Boot and shoe cut stock...	2,885	5,503	$254	$422	$168	66.1
Boot and shoe uppers.. ...	437	1,708	389	525	136	34.9
Boots and shoes, factory product.................	111,152	139,333	386	476	90	23.3
Boots and shoes, rubber...	4,662	9,264	315	428	113	35.8
Boxes, cigar............ ..	2,365	5,537	316	385	69	21.8
Boxes, fancy and paper...	9,678	19,954	245	344	99	40.4
Boxes, wooden packing...	7,722	13,922	358	465	107	29.8
Brass castings and brass finishings........	6,237	11,903	437	581	144	32.9
Brassware	1,142	7,518	360	539	179	49.7
Cigar molds..............	76	142	421	474	53	12.5
Clay and pottery products	10,221	20 296	352	499	147	41.7
Clothing, men's...........	160,813	243,857	285	456	171	60.0
Clothing, women's, factory product.................	25,192	42,008	264	447	183	69.3
Cordage and twine........	5,435	12,799	286	354	68	23.7
Cotton goods.............	185,472	221,585	245	313	68	27.7
Dentists' materials........	490	1,214	485	714	229	47.2
Electrical apparatus and supplies	1,271	9,485	537	565	28	5.2
Envelopes.....	1,204	2,501	285	423	138	48.4
Foundry and machine shop products..............	145,351	247,754	453	598	145	32.0
Furniture, including cabinet making, repairing and upholstering.... ...	52,087	78,667	417	547	130	31.1
Gas and lamp fixtures.....	3,069	5,530	478	649	171	35.7
Glass cutting, staining and ornamenting	1,586	3,794	445	658	213	47.8
Gloves and mittens	7,697	8,669	215	358	143	66.5
Gold and silver reducing and refining, not from the ore.............	304	966	587	798	211	35.9
Hats and caps, not including wool hats..........	17,240	27,193	384	518	134	34.8
House furnishing goods not elsewhere specified......	592	3,667	366	485	119	32.5
Instruments, professional and scientific	1,099	2,371	535	677	142	26.5
Iron and steel nails and spikes, cut and wrought, including wire nails.....	2,910	17,116	431	456	25	5.8
Iron and steel pipe, wrought..............	5,210	12,064	343	484	141	41.1
Iron work, architectural and ornamental...	1,934	18,672	436	640	204	46.7

INDUSTRY.	NUMBER OF EMPLOYEES		YEARLY WAGES		AMOUNT OF INCREASE.	PER CENT. OF INCREASE
	1880	1890	1880	1890		
Jewelry and instrument cases...................	138	1,038	$369	$566	197	53.3
Jute and jute goods.......	525	1,212	270	323	53	19.6
Leather goods.............	1,036	3,074	443	476	33	7.4
Leather, patent and enameled	22	2,087	581	648	67	11.5
Lithographing and engraving...................	4,322	10,590	533	674	131	24.5
Lock and gunsmithing....	887	2,560	415	586	171	41.2
Mattresses and spring beds	2,394	7,337	362	498	136	37.5
Millinery and lace goods..	6,555	11,827	253	461	208	82.2
Musical instruments, pianos and materials....	6,575	13,057	709	715	6	00.8
Oil, cottonseed and cake .	3,319	6,301	265	302	37	13.9
Oil, lubricating...........	413	1,072	503	817	314	62.4
Plumbing and gas fitting..	9,084	42,513	492	676	184	37.4
Printing and publishing...	58,478	165,227	522	635	113	21.6
Printing materials........	191	866	517	561	44	8.5
Pulp, wood...............	1,209	2,830	367	434	67	18.2
Rubber and elastic goods..	6,268	9,802	366	460	94	25.6
Shirts...................	25,687	32,750	210	326	116	55.2
Showcases................	692	1,500	475	584	109	22.9
Silk and silk goods........	31,337	50,913	291	386	95	32.6
Silversmithing............	131	314	585	807	222	37.9
Silverware................	1,029	2,306	656	701	45	6.8
Sporting goods............	1,401	2,199	293	401	108	36.8
Stationery goods not elsewhere specified.........	3,117	4,790	372	473	101	27.1
Steam fittings and heating apparatus..............	2,474	11,779	527	644	117	22.2
Stereotyping and electrotyping	642	1,475	486	724	38	7.8
Tools not elsewhere specified.....................	3,151	7,095	472	584	112	23.7
Trunks and valises........	4,534	6,785	394	517	123	31.2
Type founding............	1,986	2,172	482	645	163	33.8
Umbrellas and canes.....	3,608	6,863	321	466	145	45.1
Watch and clock materials	278	503	309	519	210	67.9
Watch cases	1,758	3,869	555	547	8*	1.4*
Watch, clock and jewelry repairing...............	1,657	3,647	523	637	114	21.7
Watches	3,346	6,675	511	552	41	8.0
Wirework, including wire rope and cable.........	4,459	7,917	383	503	120	31.3

* Decrease.

From this table it will be seen that in every industry, instead of the number of laborers practically having diminished, without exception it has largely increased, and this not by increased competition and lowering of wages but always with increased wages. In other words, the labor displacement has not only not been permanent, but the demand for labor in each industry has been increased and wages advanced.

Cotton manufacture is no exception to this rule. The table just cited gives the comparison only from 1880 to 1890, but if we either follow the investigation farther back, or bring it down to the present, we find that the same general tendency continues. For instance, in 1831 there were only 62,208 laborers employed in cotton manufacture in this country, and these were in small factories with old-fashioned looms, without a weft fork or stop action of any kind, and the operatives could only mind two looms. With the improvements of machinery, which have always been displacing laborers or else doing more work with the same number of laborers, the number of operatives in that industry, instead of diminishing, has constantly increased. In 1850 it rose to 92,286 ; in 1860 to 122,028 ; in 1870 to 135,369 ; in 1880 to 185,472 ; in 1890 to 221,585, and the number is still larger now, but the facts for the whole country have not been recently collected. During the process of this displacement, from 1830 to 1880, the number of spindles operated by each laborer increased nearly three times, the product per spindle increased one-fourth, (which shows that they went very much faster), the product per dollar invested was doubled, the cost or price of cotton cloth to the community was reduced about sixty per cent., the consumption of cotton cloth by the community per capita of the population increased over one hundred per cent., and wages more than doubled.

According to the Massachusetts Labor Report for 1885 (page 187), the general wages of mill operatives in Maine, New Hampshire, Massachusetts, Rhode Island and Connecticut from 1831 to 1880 rose 115 per cent. From 1880 to 1890 the same tendency has continued; looms have been speeded, mules have been lengthened, ring frames have been substituted for mules, the tendency of displacement has gone on, and yet the number of operatives has not diminished, but has largely increased, and wages in the entire cotton industry have risen, according to the census, more than twenty-five per cent

If we take the report of the most extensive investigation into wages and prices that has ever been made at any time in any country,—the United States Senate Report of 1893,—similar facts are revealed. This report shows that in the industry where the least labor-displacing machinery was introduced, such as agriculture, stock raising, etc., prices have risen, in a number of instances 100 per cent. and very generally from 30 to 70 per cent.; while on the other hand the tables give 140 groups of manufactured products in the making of which labor-displacing machinery has largely been introduced, and in all of these prices have fallen, varying from 6 to 40 per cent., and some as much as 70 per cent. What is also quite marked is the fact that in these industries where labor-displacing machinery and organization have been introduced, not only have prices fallen but the number of laborers employed has increased and wages have greatly risen.

This report shows that the average wages from 1860 to 1891 rose 68 per cent. (from 1840 to 1890 wages rose 204 per cent.) and the purchasing power of a day's work increased slightly over 72 per cent. In other words, through this very labor-displacing process, in lessening the cost of production, increasing the number of employments, lowering the price of the product, and increasing wages, the purchasing power of labor, which really represents the social welfare of the laborer, increased 24 per cent. every ten years from 1860 to 1890.

The farther we pursue the history of this development the clearer it becomes that the introduction of labor-displacing machinery does not tend to increase enforced idleness, but on the contrary it is a temporary displacement and not a permanent discharge of labor that takes place. The economic reason for this I have already explained,—the growing market for products, enlarging the demand for labor. It is, therefore, the height of unwisdom—in fact it is direct resistance to progress and social improvement—to oppose the introduction of improved machinery. In the case of New England such action would be specially injurious, because the cotton industry in New England is in an exceptionally critical condition by virtue of the migratory character of the industry, to which I have referred. If the laborers resist the introduction of new looms, they will stop the possibility of the industry in New England holding its own with the South. This must necessarily cause a fiercer struggle between the laborers and the corporations, which will result either, as I have said, in New England largely losing the business or the laborers moving away and an inferior class coming, or else another reduction of wages and another protracted strike, which is only another way of destroying the industry and disrupting New England labor conditions.

If, on the other hand, the laborers would welcome the new machines the capitalists would save probably half the cost of weaving. The new looms require a larger investment than the old, but, if the laborers operate sixteen to twenty instead of from six to eight, the cost of weaving would be reduced at least fifty per cent. after allowing for the fact that a little more expensive cotton would have to be used with the new device. This would create a profit margin for the corporations, and they would naturally, if the laborers intelligently make the demand (and they ought to), be willing to give a part of this to the laborers. A concession that could easily be given by the corporations would amount to from $1.00 to $2.00 a week more than they can get with the present looms, and with the new devices the working of the sixteen or eighteen looms will be about as easy as the six or eight. The result would be a net increase of wages for the laborers of fully another ten per cent. This can be secured with little or no difficulty if the new machines are used. Moreover, there are many other rearrangements that can be made and would more readily be made if the operatives would consent to it, in the different departments of the mills, by which more machinery could be minded by a sub-division of the work such that less ground had to be traversed in doing the same thing. If this also were permitted without resistance, something of a rise of wages, which would simply be a division with the laborers of the economy

secured, could be obtained in nearly all the departments of the mills.

If labor organizations mean anything they mean
uniting the strength and educating the intelligence of
the laboring people.   They should not be less intelligent and less informed than the capitalists or the community.   Their welfare is the welfare of the community, the increase of their income can only be associated with increase of productive power and permanence of industrial success.   In all the methods that
promote this end it is the interest of the laborers and
the community, as much as of the capitalists, intelligently to cooperate; but of course always cooperate
on the condition that the laborers share in the gain.

Instead, therefore, of opposing the introduction of
new machines, it is the laborer's interest always and
everywhere to encourage their introduction, but always
to see to it that though the price per unit of work is
lessened the aggregate amount the laborer receives for
a day's work is increased with the use of every new
device.   If the laborers will take the attitude of demanding a share in the increased product, instead of
preventing the introduction of the machines by which
it is to come, they will not only promote industrial development but greatly accelerate the movement which
gives them higher wages, shorter hours, cheaper
wealth and altogether more intelligent, harmonious re-
lations with the community and the employing class.

The following is one of the questions asked at the
close of this lecture, and the reply thereto :

Question.   Suppose you were a member of one of
the trade unions in the New England factory towns,

and this proposition came up very definitely of what action should be taken about the new machines, when it was known that they would throw out one-third to one-half of the members of the union while those remaining were to get more pay. If you were one of those who were going to be retained at higher pay, how could you vote for what you knew was going to throw out half of the others entirely?

Answer. That is a very practical question, yet it is one with which the individual operatives have to deal. If I were a member of the union I should endeavor to get my organization to control and modify, as far as possible, this readjustment. If opposing the introduction of the new machines would in any way be a benefit I might favor that, but since it clearly is not and the improved machinery will come in any event, and if resisted will bring greater catastrophe when it does come, direct opposition is clearly a futile thing. As a member of the union, therefore, I would not advocate that. Since the new machines must be adopted as the only means of escaping the crushing competition which would force the displacement of factories, and perhaps another effort to reduce wages or else the introduction of a cheaper class of labor from Canada or Europe, I would endeavor to use the power of organization to mitigate the personal hardships of the readjustments.

The laborers ought first to decide that they will accept the new machines, and then enter into a rational understanding with the corporations as to the amount of increase of aggregate wages the new machines would yield. Then, all who were employed upon the new looms should be expected to pay a special assessment into the union, constituting perhaps half or a certain proportion of their increase, as an out-of-work fund to be used in aiding dislocated weavers to obtain new situations in other places, or in new mills now being erected either in Massachusetts or elsewhere.

It must be remembered that the introduction of the new machines is not coming in a night. Only some of the mills will adopt the new looms at first. Many will postpone it because they are not ready to make the increased investment, and so the transition will come somewhat gradually; and if the unions would use a part of the increased wages obtained by the new machines to aid their fellow-members in relocating either in other places or industries, the direct hardship of the readjustment would be greatly lessened.

Another thing I should advocate if I were a member of the union would be the speedy adoption of effective restriction of immigration, so that corporations could not have the opportunity of bringing in new immigrants for the purpose of this readjusting operation, but that all the new mills which are erected should at least perform the function of absorbing the labor being displaced in the transition. I would also advocate the enlisting of trade unions throughout the country in an active movement for reducing the hours of labor in the South to the level of those in Massachusetts, so that the long-hour workday should not present a barrier to the emigration of laborers from New England to the southern states. In both these movements the operatives might fairly expect to have the cooperation and financial aid of the employers.

XII

THE TIN-PLATE TRUST *

THE manufacture of tin plate is one of the recent industries which have been brought into existence in this country exclusively by a protective tariff. Prior to 1890 there was not a pound of tin plate manufactured in this country. We imported all our supply, free of duty. Under the McKinley Law (1890) a duty of 2⅕ cents a pound was placed upon manufactured tin plates. This immediately had the effect of establishing the industry in this country, and we now produce our entire supply, foreigners being unable to compete with American producers in the American market. The product since July 1st, 1891, has been as follows:

July 1 to December 31, 1891, (half year)	2,236,743
January 1 to December 31, 1892.........	42,119,192
January 1 to December 31, 1893.........	123,606,707
January 1 to December 31, 1894.........	166,343,409
January 1 to December 31, 1895.........	225,004,869
January 1 to December 31, 1896.........	369,229,796
January 1 to December 31, 1897.........	574,759,628
January 1 to December 31, 1898.........	732,290,285

Total product for 7½ years....2,235,590,629

* Published in *Gunton's Magazine* of May 1899.

Before the McKinley Law was passed, when tin-plate was on the free list, it cost $5.10 per box. After the industry got well under way in this country the price rapidly fell, at one time touching $2.75 a box. In 1894 the Wilson Bill reduced the tariff on tin-plate to 1¼ cents. Under the Dingley Bill, of 1897, the tariff was raised to 1½ cents, but the price did not rise. Indeed, it has remained so low that no foreign tin can come in.

In the fall of 1898 the price in hundred-pound boxes was $3.00 a box. This price was regarded as very low, yielding very little profit for the best concerns and none at all for poorer ones, and a loss for some of the poorest. Competition among the various factories that the tariff had called into existence was so severe that steps were taken to reorganize the industry into a trust, by which all the factories became parts of one concern. Almost immediately after the trust was organized the price of tin-plates went up from $3.00 to $4.00 a box. This very naturally caused consternation among the consumers and a feeling of indignation in the community that the trust was using the power of its new organization to impose upon the public, and, instead of giving the consumers a part of the benefit of the economy created by the larger organization, that it was acting the part of a monopoly and charging one-third more, merely for its profits.

In the March issue of this magazine, in an article " The Era of Trusts," attention was called to this fact. It was suggested that if the managers of the tin-plate trust had no better appreciation of the treatment that industry had received at the hands of the public in the form of a protective tariff, upon which its very existence depended, than to use its organization to tax the community by monopoly prices, its products should at once be put upon the free list; and, in fact, that congress should pass a law empowering the secretary of the treasury to put upon the free list the products of any trust that uses its reorganization to put up prices. In nearly all cases where legitimate trusts have been organized and great economies accomplished, the management has had the good sense to lower the price and so give the community a share of the advantages due to the superior methods of organization. Hence the fact that the tin-plate trust was an exception to this and put the price up over 30 per cent. seemed to be an example of bad business policy.

Subsequent investigation into the facts of the case, however, shows that the managers of the tin-plate industry are not quite so unwise as this rise in price would seem to indicate. Of course, in passing upon all such cases we should be careful to hold the trust responsible only for what it does. It has frequently happened when the price of petroleum has tilted upwards that the trust has been condemned as the greedy cause, whereas a little investigation would show that it was due to a rise in crude oil. The same has more than once been true of sugar.

This happens to be true at least in part of tin plate. It should be remembered that the tin plate manufacturers, now the trust, simply buy the pig tin and the steel bars. They roll the bars into plates, and otherwise prepare them, and put on the tin coating. In other words, pig tin and steel bars are their raw materials, both of which they buy. Pig tin is all imported, duty free, and steel bars are largely manufactured here.

Pig tin has risen from 12¾ cents to 25 cents a pound, or over 96 per cent. The price of steel billets, out of which the plates are made, has risen from $14.50 to $25.00 a ton, or 72.4 per cent. Allowing about 5 per cent. for waste in converting the billets into plates, this is equivalent to a rise of $10.50 on 1,900 pounds. Therefore, the price of the 2½ pounds of pig tin used in the manufacture of 100 pounds of plates has risen 30.6 cents, and the price of the steel billets used in 100 pounds of tin plate has risen 54.8 cents, making a rise in the cost of the two elements of raw material of 85.4 cents per box of tin plate. Before the rise, the steel billets used in making a box of tin plate cost 74.1 cents, and the pig tin cost 31.9 cents, or just $1.06 per box. Therefore the rise in raw materials in a hundred-pound box has been 80 per cent.

When the price of the finished plates was $3.00, the remaining $1.94 above the cost of raw materials was made up of labor, fuel and miscellaneous expenses. The fuel cost is about 5 cents per box of tin, and if we allow an equal amount for taxes and insurance respectively, which is more than ample, 20 cents for fixed salaries—a very high estimate indeed—, and 9 cents for depreciation and incidental expenses not enumerated, the remaining $1.50 represents labor cost,—including the salaries of clerks, etc. On this there has been a rise of 11 per cent., or 16½ cents per box. Adding this to the 85.4 cents rise in the price of raw materials makes a total rise of $1.02 a box in the cost of manufacture, due to the rise of wages and in the price of raw materials.

Of course, the $3.00 a box for which the tin plates

were sold in 1898 did not all represent cost of production to the most successful factories. There were a few of the best concerns that were making a profit when business was at its worst and prices at their lowest; but with the poorer mills, or those producing at the greatest cost, all of the $3.00 represented cost of production. They were receiving no profits, and some of them were working at a loss. This is always the case in competitive business, but it was especially the case during 1896, 1897 and 1898. That is to say, under all normal competitive conditions those producing at the greatest cost work without profit, and their cost is correctly reflected in the selling price. Usually these producers are comparatively few, but in 1896, 1897 and 1898 they were numerous; some of the poorest, as just observed, being compelled to work at a loss. Since these dearest producers always determine the market price it is perfectly correct to estimate the $3.00 as representing the cost of producing the plate, not including any profit, as those whose cost really determine the price received no profit.

Strictly speaking, then, the rise in wages and raw material in the manufacture of tin-plate has been slightly more, or at least fully equal to, the increase in the price since the trust was organized. The increased economies of the trust probably amount to more than this. They have probably converted what was a loss to some, no profit to many, and a small profit to only a few into a more liberal profit for all, and it may fairly be expected that the trust will share this undivided profit with the community before long in a further reduction of prices. We are glad, however, to be able to believe that whatever increased profit the trust is now making it is not getting it out of the rise of price.

It is worth noting in this connection that the price of tin-plate, with the increase of 11 per cent. in wages, is still $1.10 a box less than it was when we relied on foreign supply for all our tin-plate under free importation. What has really been accomplished is this : the tin-plate industry has been transferred to this country, whatever profits there are now go to American investors, the wages expended in that industry are distributed to American laborers, these wages have been increased since the trust was organized 11 per cent., the producers are undoubtedly making a good profit, and still the product is sold to American consumers at $1.10 a box, or 22 per cent. less than before the tariff was adopted and the trust organized.

XIII.

THE TETHER OF LARGE FORTUNES*

THE retirement of Mr. Andrew Carnegie from business, with the announcement that he intends to devote the remainder of his life to giving away his fortune of $150,000,000, has given rise to a good deal of discussion of millionaires and their fortunes. Mr. Carnegie has some rather unique characteristics. For a time he took considerable pains to announce in different ways that it is very unfortunate for a young man to be born with a fortune, and that it is not creditable for a man to die rich, because by so doing he really handicaps his sons or other relatives to whom the fortune passes. Since the advent of his little daughter, however, this particular phase of his philosophy of wealth has been less emphasized, and it would almost seem as if the little girl were in some danger of being terribly handicapped.

Yet, as a part of that idea and not inconsistent with it, Mr. Carnegie is credited with announcing that in retiring from the cares of business he is going to devote himself to becoming a public benefactor, in giving away his immense fortune. To perform this task wisely may indeed be quite as difficult as it was to earn it. In accumulating a fortune by successfully

---

conducting productive enterprise, a person is sure to benefit the community in ways that are economic and permanent, because the helpful influences which arise from productive industry operate silently and unconsciously through the distributive forces of society. Millions of new wealth may thus be created and distributed in wages and profits and other forms of earnings which are sure to find healthful lodgment throughout the community. But when a single individual undertakes to make a business of distributing a hundred or more millions, there is danger of considerable wasteful misplacement. Yet this step of Mr. Carnegie's has met with a good deal of approval, and, but for the misfortune of the Homestead affair, which will probably never be entirely erased from his shield, Mr. Carnegie would receive well-nigh universal applause.

There is a very strong feeling abroad, and it seems to be growing, that capitalists, and especially multi-millionaires, are a menace to public welfare, in grabbing the world's wealth to the impoverishment of the great mass of the community. Hence Mr. Carnegie's new departure—for it is about the first case of the kind that ever occurred—is regarded as an example to be emulated.

It is quite an open question whether, if all millionaires should follow Mr. Carnegie's example, they would really render better service to the public. He made a very sensible remark on this subject when he said the reason so few rich men retire from business is that while they have plenty to retire from they have little to retire to. In other words, their lives have been so absorbed in the pursuits of industry, out of which their fortunes have been made, that there is not enough in other walks of life to attract them, or even to make life tolerable to them if they should leave business altogether. This is very true. The men of great business affairs are tied to their business long after they have made adequate fortunes, because they cannot leave it. Life would be a burden to them if they did. In short, to continue in business is the only way for them to make life worth living.

This brings up a side of the life of great business men and millionaires that is generally overlooked by those who insist that the industrial magnates who control great enterprises are " gobbling all the benefits of civilization." A little consideration of this side of the problem reveals the fact that, after all, even millionaires can only really take unto themselves the amount of wealth that their social life and character can absorb. Very few of them can actually absorb more than $25,000 a year. They may spend $100,000, but they give it largely to other people ; the rest of the income from their millions goes directly or indirectly to society. As the capitalist cannot use by his own social absorption but a small portion of his fortune, the rest must be invested productively or it is in danger of slipping from him. In reality, both the millionaire and his wealth, outside of the little he can absorb socially, are devoted in spite of themselves to the service of the public. By virtue of a life habit, acquired in the creation of his fortune, he has become tethered to the service of production. He has become so closely tethered to business that he does not even take on so much of the socializing influence of civilization, does not really absorb so much of the progress of society, does not, therefore, enjoy so much of the mellowing and sweetening influences of culture, as many others who have not a hundredth or a thousandth part of his wealth. In short, there are even whole classes who get far more of the best results of the wealth of modern society than do the capitalist millionaires themselves, who have become the closely tethered servants, not to say slaves, of productive fortunes.

It may be said with some truth that in many instances these servants of fortunes are really dwarfed on the best side of their nature, and in not a few instances have become indifferent to the great ethical and social movements which are making for a higher type of human life. This is frequently made a subject of criticism. They are denounced as mean and selfish, illiberal and oppressive. But it is more correct to regard them as victims of an exacting industrial life. By their very superior capacity as industrial organizers, developers of the world's resources, by which wealth is made cheaper and more abundant and the whole standard of life raised, they have become tethered to a duty from which they cannot escape. The notion that millionaires monopolize the enjoyment of their millions is wholly unwarranted. They really get the benefit only of a diminishing proportion of an increasing product. In proportion as their fortune increases their exclusive enjoyment of it becomes relatively smaller. Whatever else may be said, it is obvious that the great millionaire capitalists of modern times are drudges to their fortunes, and indirectly to the community.

From an immediate moral point of view it may seem to be a misfortune that the class who contribute most to the possibility of civilization should thus be dwarfed by the process, but this seems to have been inevitable under the circumstances. Thus far it appears to have been an inexorable edict of evolution that the efficient few should render exceptional service for the benefit of the less efficient many. In no other way could modern progress have been possible. The application of science through the use of machinery, which periodically has involved the reorganization of industry into larger and more economical concerns, has necessarily brought with it more and more exacting demands upon the managing captains. This movement toward greater productive efficiency, which every hour is increasing the world's wealth, has practically involved forcing successful capitalists into a business groove, which is the dwarfing process complained of. It is a rare exception to find a man really broad, generous, public-spirited and well rounded-out at the same time that he is building up his fortune. His sons may be broader, more liberal and highly cultivated ; the community is progressing, but he is immersed in the responsibility of successfully conducting an enterprise which makes this very broadening progress possible for others.

The capitalist is not only a servant in the highest sense to civilization, but his very service so shapes his habits and desires as to make it more difficult for him to escape than to continue the drudgery. It is very doubtful if one per cent. of capitalists to-day could retire from business at sixty-five without being less useful and less happy than they would be by continuing in the harness.

Of course, if industrial progress had this effect upon all the community it would be disastrous indeed. It would neutralize its own benefits. But, fortunately, in this case as in the case of labor displacement, the sacrifice of personal disadvantage is limited to a few and the benefits are extended to the many, so that the great mass whose tastes, habits and life create the standard of civilization and the environment for each individual are helped by the process.

It is true that this warping or dwarfing influence is a feature almost peculiar to modern industry. At least, it has very much increased with the growth of modern methods. The farther back we go the more we find the condition where the employer was an easy-going, paternal kind of man, largely a public character, the mayor of the town, the adviser of the widow, and a sort of godfather to the community, and if we go still farther back, where there were practically no employers and everybody worked for himself, this element did not exist but barbarism was the lot of all. Neither was there any dislocation of laborers in that primitive simple state. Both these phases of seeming sacrifice have come with the colossal movement of progress. It is fortunate for society that this whole movement is concentrating the dwarfing responsibilities for the wealth-getting efforts of the world to a smaller and smaller proportion of society and distributing the results to an ever increasing number.

For instance, the wage and salary system, which is a part of this progress, harnesses a constantly increasing proportion of the workers as simple productive automatons, where their hours are prescribed, their wages fixed, the quality of their efforts specialized almost to the point of monotony. In proportion as their duties become automatic they become unexacting, and to that extent the nervous force and vital energies of the people are reserved to be let loose in the sphere of social activities in which the gratifications of the higher side of life come. In the lines where this reaches its highest perfection, the drudgery or exacting side of earning a living is measured by the hours of daily application. In proportion as these can be shortened, the world of social expansion and rounded human cultivation is enlarged. Thus, by this process, the millions are being more and more relieved from the burdensome narrow rut of life by being made irresponsible parts of the semi-automatic whole, for the successful management of which a smaller and smaller number, relatively, become responsible.

Of course, in the philosophic consideration of the case the question arises, will this always be necessary ? Will progress always demand the sacrifice of the most painstaking experts in the productive life? It would seem not. The tendency of this movement is manifestly to organize, systematize and centralize, so that ultimately a large amount of automatic momentum will be established, and this will bring relief even to those at the helm. When the machinery and organization in an industry has reached approximate perfection, or a stage where great revolutions are no longer possible, what has heretofore required practical genius to direct becomes an established order, each part of which almost takes care of itself. When the presence or direction of no given individual is indispensable to the movement of the whole, when the death of the guiding genius would not disrupt the working of the concern ; when that point is reached —and it has already been reached in some industries—

the capitalist or the great captain of industry will become more perfunctory, less tightly tethered to duty, and in common with the rest of the community may take on more of the broader and refining side of life and be less immersed in the drudgery of business.

But in the evolutionary process which is now going on they are the drudges of industry. In a broad view of the subject, therefore, great capitalists in pursuing a seemingly narrow life, absorbed by business and dominated by margins and markets, are rendering the best service to society of which they are capable, and the fact that they appear to find the highest gratification in the pursuit of industry is in this age at least to the greatest advantage of civilization.

It is a misfortune that the function of the capitalist class is so much misunderstood. It leads to a great deal of adverse criticism of their conduct, and tends to sour them towards public interests. They are made to feel that they are hunted and censured for their success. They are kept constantly under the harrow of public criticism and censure, which tends to make their social life even less attractive and endurable than it otherwise would be, and here the capitalists as a class help to intensify this social antagonism by too frequently ignoring and defying public sentiment. They must learn that, right or wrong, the public is master ; that public opinion is the opinion that rules and will rule ; and that it is a part of good economic investment, a part of wise industrial statesmanship, to devote a part of the earnings of their enterprises to the education of the people, to a broader and more philosophic understanding of the capitalist's relation to society and society's relation to capitalistic enterprises. It would be a mistake if the capitalists should evolve the theory that the true way is to ignore the public till they get rich and then retire to spend their riches for public purposes. By this process they would succeed in being disliked as capitalists and doubted as philanthropists.

The true function of a capitalist is to be a successful organizer and director of industry, and devote a part of the proceeds to movements of education and public improvement as he goes along. In that way his contributions are likely to be good investments, involving little waste and producing the maximum results. In most cases it is safe to say that the great fortune would do more good to be left in productive enterprises than to be distributed in great lumps in any lines of philanthropy. What is needed is that the people should understand the function of the capitalist, and that the capitalist should understand the need of more liberal public improvements. In this way an altogether more harmonious relation between capital and the community would be evolved, and the capitalist do his best work for civilization, make his best contributions to public improvement, and get a larger and larger personal advantage out of pursuing an important, and what has hitherto been an exhausting, life of business drudgery.

XIV.

POWERS AND PERILS OF THE NEW TRUSTS *

TEN or a dozen years have now elapsed since the trust movement in this country began to assume really formidable proportions ; yet the material conditions of the people gradually improve, and the republic still endures. Probably no great natural movement or tendency in the world's history ever brought out such widespread protests and dire prophecies of disaster as this modern tendency of capitalistic combination. It has been declaimed against, preached against, flayed in the press, denounced in all political platforms, and attacked by professors of political economy with all their resources of scholarly exposition, showing the industrial despotism and thraldom of the masses that was sure to come, and uttering solemn warnings. "Combinations in restraint of trade" have been outlawed by nearly every state in the Union, and even by national legislation as far as it could be made to apply to the subject. Yet the trusts march on, and the laws step one side, because in not one case out of a hundred is it possible to show that they are combinations "in restraint of trade"; until, it is estimated, about four billion dollars of the capital invested in productive industry in this country has now come

---

* Published in *Gunton's Magazine* of June 1899.

under some form of trust organization, and more than one and one-half billions of this during the last five months.

Is it not a little strange that, in spite of all this, the long promised cataclysm has not yet arrived,—in fact, seems farther off than ever? Was there ever anything so remarkable in the world's industrial history as this tremendous, silent revolution that has been going on right under our eyes, yet so smoothly and naturally as to create hardly a ripple of disturbance in the great economic round of daily production and consumption? The average man would hardly have had cause to suspect what was taking place, but for the deluge of newspaper warnings. True, as the consolidation went on, some factories, generally the poorer ones, were closed down; but that had happened over and over again in the natural course of free competition. Again, employees were discharged in many instances, but that too was no novelty. It had always occurred whenever a concern failed or a plant suspended operations because of inability to keep in the race. The laborers under such circumstances have always had to seek employment in other establishments; some of them, perhaps, remaining in idleness until the growth of business created new demands for labor. Hard as it is, there has been relatively no more difficulty about this readjusting process in recent years than formerly; in fact, at present the percentage of non-employment is very small indeed, and the question is chiefly one of finding the right sort of men for the different kinds of work to be done. As to ruin of small competitors, it has actually been a great cause of complaint against many recent trusts that they

have taken in and saved groups of old and poor concerns that would shortly have gone to the wall any-
way, making the productive part of the trust carry
the burden of these unprofitable plants.

Neither in respect to small industries nor their employees, therefore, have the trusts brought any new
and unusual hardships. From the community's standpoint, it is notable that during the past year the
growth of trusts and revival of business prosperity
have come along hand in hand. Whether there be
any connection between the two or not, it is clear that
the one has in no way had the effect of preventing or
destroying the other.

This has become so conspicuous, staring everybody
in the face, that public sentiment in many quarters is
changing towards the whole problem. Old standard
newspapers, the very ones that have persistently attacked the trust movement for years, are coming to
discuss the matter in a markedly different spirit. Lec-
turers on the subject need not now quite exhaust the
dictionary of vituperation in order to get a hearing.
Still, opposition has by no means died out. No political party as yet dares descend to mildness even, in
its references to trusts. "Down with them!" is to
be the chief rallying cry next year of one of the great
political parties at least, and the other will meet this
by trying to show that it (the party) has done more to
stamp out trusts than has its opponent. Each party
must be a St. George to some dragon, and what more
convenient dragon is at hand than the trust? What
would a political speech amount to without some
hideous oppressor writhing on the rack, and the orator
turning the screw?

But the opposition is not all mere "ranting," by any means. There is a well defined feeling among a large group of people, not usually moved by mere prejudice, that we are rapidly drifting into a condition extremely perilous to industrial and political freedom and progress, even though these results are not yet manifest. They ask, in alarm, whether we shall not soon reach a point where, all competition being killed, the trusts will throw off all restraint and manipulate prices, wages and legislation precisely to suit themselves. They seem to see every avenue of individual effort closed, especially to men of small means, and the whole community reduced to the status of wage earners who will have no choice between serving the trusts and facing starvation. They are possessed of a dread that the outcome of all this will be one universal trust, controlling and disposing of everything like a medieval despotism.

These are the powers commonly supposed to lie in the hands of the trusts, or that will lie in their hands absolutely if the movement continues much longer.

Now let us see what ground, if any, there is for all this alarm. Are the trusts all-powerful, or likely to become so? Before we can answer this we need, first of all, to find the source of what power they do possess. It is not in any arbitrary ability permanently to raise prices, reduce wages, and control the output. Many foolish attempts have been made to do exactly these things, and, except where there was some real economic justification for the step taken, they have disastrously failed. Several wheat "corners," the whisky trust, copper trust, cordage trust, the nail and other attempted combinations in different branches of the iron industry, are examples of what comes of economic folly. Now, when these experiences are contrasted with the steady and permanent success of trusts which have adopted the opposite policy of permanent economic improvements, reduction of prices, and fair dealing with employees, it furnishes a very powerful object lesson to new trusts. Some, of course, have not profited by it yet, but they will encounter the penalties of their predecessors unless they do.

It is not surprising that this should be so. A mere trade agreement between a group of concerns does not and cannot abolish competition. "Corners" cannot succeed. They must go on buying up every new competitor that appears in the field, but this cannot continue very long without completely destroying the profitableness of the business. It was this, chiefly, that brought about the collapse of the "corners" just enumerated.

The threat of new outside competition is more constant and powerful to-day than ever before. No trust organization can safely ignore it. One of the chief reasons why it is becoming so important a factor is the rapid growth of our surplus capital. Industry has been so profitable in this country that we have gradually accumulated a great fund of surplus, and, instead of trying to borrow money abroad, our capitalists are actually seeking opportunities to place foreign loans. Interest rates have steadily declined. Railroad after railroad has been going through financial reorganization, refunding its bonded indebtedness at from one to three per cent. lower rates than were previously paid. Capital, instead of being difficult to obtain, is eagerly

13

watching every opportunity for profitable investment. This means that nobody can have any absolute control over prices. A new method or invention in productive processes, if obtained by some actual or possible rival, is likely to undermine a trust at almost any time. Their only safety lies in maintaining the lead in introducing every possible improvement and economy, and thereby keeping the price on a steadily downward movement which competitors cannot follow.

A mistaken policy on the part of a vast industrial concern is a far more serious matter than the common daily errors in the conduct of a small business. That it is a very serious matter to maintain the constant supremacy of these immense concerns is shown by the necessity they are under of securing as officers and managers men of the greatest energy and ability that money can find. Indeed, it is pure folly to imagine that great power can exist without great responsibility, or can increase without making discretion and just conduct more and more essential. The great rough balance that exists everywhere in nature and keeps it right side up and in stable equilibrium operates also in economics, and prevents any permanent, one-sided monopoly of power and privilege.

The situation to-day in this trust matter shows how true this is. We have been so impressed by the enormous growth of the trusts themselves as almost to overlook a fact of equal importance,—that competition also has been growing more and more keen, even though it is fighting now with larger weapons, and not with a multitude of staves and spears as under the system of small individual industry. The Standard Oil Company, perhaps, comes as near being an industrial monopoly as any concern in this country, yet it has either never cared to or never been able to obtain control of some twenty-five or thirty independent refining companies, more than fifteen of which have from $100,000 to $1,000,000 capital and are quoted in the standard commercial rate books as establishments of good credit. Should this company, through some strange freak of management, reverse its established policy and try to restore the oil prices of several years ago, there is no doubt but that capital would be put into many of these outside plants, and into new oil fields, and powerful competing industries built up. The Standard maintains its position only by keeping prices at a point so low that only a few well situated outsiders can compete.

The sugar trust for several years after its formation had practically no competition. Now, however, for a year or more a fierce fight has been in progress between the sugar trust and the Arbuckles, which seems no nearer conclusion than ever. But, it is stated on quite definite official authority, that if at any time these competitors should combine there are at least two new syndicates ready and waiting to enter the field, one operating in Maryland and the other in New York. It is even more difficult to monopolize this business than the refining of petroleum. The one fact of the rapid growth of free capital seeking investment is a force, tending to keep all such industries at the point of greatest efficiency and lowest prices, infinitely more powerful than all the legislation that could be devised for that purpose.

Much the same situation is developing in the case of paper manufacture. About seventy-five or eighty per cent. of the producing capacity of the country was brought into the recently organized paper trust, but there is already vigorous competition outside, and prospect of rapid growth of new independent concerns. The *New York Journal of Commerce and Commercial Bulletin*, a pronounced anti-trust paper, is authority for this information. According to the *Shoe and Leather Reporter* precisely the same condition exists with reference to the leather and rubber goods trusts. "There are a number of outside companies," it says, "who are holding their own and maintaining a high standing in the trade."

Even in lines of business that seem to be in their nature as nearly monopolistic as it is possible to be, there has recently been an unprecedented amount of competition. The severe fight among the gas companies in New York city has brought about a reduction, by some of the companies, to 65 cents per thousand feet, and by others to 50 cents, while the uniform price before was $1.10. It is not probable that this state of affairs will continue long, because the price quoted is probably just about at the cost point of production. A consolidation may be effected and a somewhat higher uniform rate established, but it is safe to predict that never again will the former price be reached. If it gets above 85 or 90 cents, there is really nothing to prevent the entrance of still other competitors, as in the present case, anxious to share the profits at that rate. This has not been confined to New York. Other cities have recently secured considerable reduction in gas rates, and still others are considering propositions from competing companies to furnish gas much cheaper than at present.

This is also true in the case of street railway transportation. The steady tendency is to give us better cars, faster time, and cheaper service through the increased mileage covered by a five-cent fare, and extension of transfer arrangements. In New York this movement has been so extensive lately that the suburban movement is really taking on enormous proportions. Competition between the elevated and surface lines, added to the pressure of the public demand, has, within the last few months, produced most important results. The elevated railway is to change its motive power to electricity, equip its line with new cars and establish express train service. The Metropolitan is continually extending the area of transfers, and now the Third Avenue road has arranged a transfer system with the Manhattan Elevated, and also with the Union trolley lines in the Bronx Borough, so that it is possible to go from the City Hall to New Rochelle on Long Island Sound for eight cents. In Brooklyn, which is the competitor of New Jersey and Westchester County for suburban business, a recent reorganization has already given more rapid and cheaper long distance service, and very soon the old engines and trains of the elevated roads are to be replaced by electric cars running on express train schedules.

If, therefore, competition does remain in active operation in some form or other, even in such cases as these, is it not an idle fear that it can ever be abolished in all the open and not naturally monopolistic industries? There is no reason whatever to suppose that the whole field can ever be monopolized in any line of industry. It may be comparatively easy to combine half or three-fourths of the large establishments in an industry, but it is immensely difficult to get a much larger proportion. The difficulty doubles and trebles with every new step toward the hundred per cent. mark, until further effort becomes altogether more costly than it is worth. It is like the old catch-problem of finding how long it would take to reach the end of a road by traveling half the remaining distance every hour. Progress at first is rapid, but obviously it is impossible ever to reach the end.

But, even if the amount of actual competition is reduced to very narrow limits, the possibility of new competition always exists; and, as we have pointed out, its probability increases with every increase in the surplus capital of the community. This is potential competition, and as industry becomes organized on a large and finely balanced scale it is not one whit less effective than the actual. Another important point is this:—potential competition, especially with respect to small employers and wage earners, is far more merciful and humane than when the warfare is actually on. We are forever hearing competition exalted and glorified almost as a sacred institution, of inestimable benefit to the entire community, but as a matter of plain, hard experience, it is only a part of the results of competition that is really beneficial. Its actual working, as between a multitude of small rivals, is attended with all manner of heartlessness and immorality, failure of employers and discharge of employees. The trust movement is tending to abolish these painful features by gathering the bulk of the concerns in various industries into large and permanent organizations. As these become thoroughly unified, the plants they control will have to keep in operation some way or other, like railroads, however the management may change. At the same time, by the force of potential competition, the eagerness of idle capital, and the threat of new inventions in the hands of outside parties, we shall get the benefit of cheaper commodities the same as if the competitive struggle and slaughter were actually going on. The present movement in both these directions is tending, at least, to give us an industrial system as nearly ideal as seems within the range of economic possibility.

The wage earner will not be injured. Alongside the organization of capital comes organization of labor, and this means more and more that industrial peace is absolutely necessary to the success of large concerns. As we have pointed out in another connection, the larger they become the greater the necessity of smooth operation and the more disastrous is interruption or strife. A prolonged strike or shut-down would be almost ruinous to very large concerns, while giving competitors a free hand in building up a rival business. This fact makes it more and more important to grant the reasonable demands of labor. Trade union organization in the hands of the laborers is a more effective weapon against large concerns even than against small ones, because the penalty they can inflict is immeasurably greater. Many large concerns appreciate this so keenly as to forestall trouble by voluntarily granting wage increases. This has been very conspicuous, lately, in the case of the steel, tin-plate and leather goods trusts.

Nor is the man of small capital to be crushed. He cannot, it is true, engage with much chance of success in many of the old established lines of manufacturing industry, but this by no means implies that be has no opportunity for individual investment. On the contrary, the very growth of corporations and trusts opens a broader field for a small investor than ever before. Perhaps he cannot start a plant of his own, but he can buy stock, however small the amount, in any one of hundreds or thousands of different enterprises and share in its management. These opportunities constantly increase. It is now possible for men of experience and peculiar skill in any special direction to gather together the large or small accumulations of hundreds of other people and carry on an industry that is much more likely to be profitable to them all than if each man tried to start a small business of his own. If a man happens to be a poor manager, the fact of owning his own little establishment is of no use or advantage to him. It is much better to succeed as a joint owner, employing trained and skilled management, than to fail as the incompetent sole proprietor of one's own business.

The fear that the trusts will finally control all legislation is equally groundless. At first, a decade or so ago, large corporations undoubtedly did exert a powerful influence in controlling legislation in certain directions, but the very fact that this was done in a few instances caused so great a reaction in public sentiment that the whole tendency has been to the opposite extreme ever since. To-day legislatures vie with each other in passing measures restricting the powers of corporations or increasing their taxation, while it is almost impossible for these concerns to get any legislation definitely in their favor. It is only necessary to look over the statute books throughout the country for the last few years to verify this. Every year sees increased anxiety on the part of legislators to make a record for anti-capitalist activity. There is not the least reason to suppose that this tendency will diminish. To just the extent that trusts fail to justify themselves to the public, or attempt unscrupulous methods either in business or in legislation, political hostility to them will continue.

Finally, we come to face this bugbear of a great universal trust which is to absorb everything and rule us by its own sweet will. Here again a very simple test reveals all the reasonable probabilities. Just as in the case of the permanence and stability of separate trusts, the limit to size and extension will be fixed by the test of greatest productive economy. If it is found that several different kinds of industries can be conducted jointly more economically, and hence more profitably to the owners and with lower prices to the public, consolidation will go on to that point, but no farther. If a combination is formed, in which the effort to handle two or more different kinds of industries under a single management proves more wasteful and awkward than the old plan, it will break down. New competition will be invited into the field, and former conditions will return. As productive methods become more and more highly specialized, and expert management more and more a real science in each different field, separation of very unlike industries becomes even more necessary to good results than formerly. An expert in the sugar refining business, for instance, if placed also in charge of piano making or cotton manufacturing, would probably hamper both those industries and perhaps before long render them unprofitable by his bungling interference. It is nearly impossible for one mind to be supremely expert in three or four different fields, and this simple limitation of human capacity prohibits the universal trust.

Not even if the actual running of each business were left to special experts, and only the general business policy put in the hands of a joint committee, would success always come. Different industries require different general business policies quite as much as different factory management. It would be hard to imagine a more inviting field for competitors than one in which, for instance, a miscellaneous collection of industries such as oil refining, cloth manufacturing, wheat growing, stock raising, railroad managing and store-keeping were in operation under the joint direction of one committee of managers, each with a different idea of business methods. Such a combination would be so grotesquely unnatural, cumbersome and inefficient that it probably could not last six months. It would be a more easy victim to innumerable outside assaults in specific lines than even the sleeping Gulliver to the Lilliputians.

Indeed, it is not altogether unlikely that after a few years there may be a dividing up even of some of the trusts already organized. Senator Depew, whose opportunities for insight into general industrial conditions are perhaps as broad as those of any man in the country, takes this view very strongly indeed, and even believes that we shall finally return to the conditions of a decade or more ago. This does not seem very probable, except in the case of useless and unwieldy combinations; but it would undoubtedly be true of any attempt to unite a large number of wholly different kinds of industries under one management. The grouping of each industry by itself seems to be the natural point of greatest economic efficiency; but if, in time, a real advantage is found in still wider combination along certain lines, that will come. These larger trusts, however, would be subject to exactly the same perils as we have shown exist at present. The difficulty and danger of moving counter to public welfare increase as the trust grows and exposes fresh points of attack. The only protection to economic vulnerableness is economic wisdom.

While the general trend of this whole movement affords no ground for sensational alarms as to its consequences, present or future, there are likely to be many serious disturbances in its progress, due to the ignorance or selfishness of individuals connected with it. This is and will be true wherever a speculative "corner" is organized to force up prices; or wherever a set of irresponsible brokers organize a highly overcapitalized trust and sell out their holdings, leaving the concern to flounder around as best it may, and perhaps fail for want of any real economic welding force within it. This is true, too, wherever either corporations or trusts try to interfere with the legitimate organization of labor or to reduce wages and exact longer hours of labor.

The great duty of the hour is to discriminate between the movement itself and the follies of individual bunglers. Most of the latter—" corners " for instance —bring their own economic penalties more promptly than any legislative ones that could be applied. In the case of stock watering, if the increased capital does not really represent a corresponding earning capacity, failure is certain. A few more experiences of this ought to be enough to prevent either the owners of industries from transferring their plants or owners of capital from loaning their money in aid of unsound reorganizations. Where capital interferes with the right of labor to organize, the law might properly step in and provide severe penalties for any attempt to black-list or intimidate wage earners, or break up their organizations, or require them to forswear trade union membership as a condition to employment. The duty of the public lies in watching these points, not in passionately opposing this great economic movement of society, which, as it gradually rids itself of error and attains its full possibilities, will give us permanent industrial efficiency and security. At the same time, the trusts must learn that after all the public, as consumer, competitor and lawmaker, is the real and final master of the situation. Whenever the people cease to share, and share liberally, in the benefits of this movement, its end is come.

XV.

THE TARIFF AND TRUSTS*

THE latest outbreak on the subject of the protective tariff and its relation to trusts was caused by Mr. H. O. Havemeyer's testimony given before the Industrial Commission on June 14th. Almost in the opening sentences of his carefully prepared and typewritten testimony he declared that: "The mother of all trusts is the customs tariff bill." This gave a new text to the anti-trust, and particularly the anti-tariff, preachers throughout the country. For political purposes, the anti-trust issue was in a rather unsafe condition. To be sure, Mr. Bryan was proclaiming loud and long against trusts. He and his friends decided to make this a prominent if not the conspicuous issue of the coming presidential campaign. But he has insisted on coupling with it the free coinage of silver at 16 to 1, which is economic dynamite to the conservative men throughout the country.

So that, in reality, every fresh boom for the anti-trust movement was a lift for free silver. Free traders, who generally favor sound money and even declare for the gold standard, would rather have trusts than take Bryan with 16 to 1. Consequently, some of the ablest among free trade journals have defended the

---

*Published in *Gunton's Magazine* of August 1899.

205

present administration, justified its foreign policy, and occasionally given a quasi-justification for large corporations, all because they are afraid of carrying grist to the Bryan mill. But Mr. Havemeyer came to their relief, in his testimony before the Industrial Commission, with the declaration that: "The mother of all trusts is the customs tariff bill." This statement has been hailed as the word of a political deliverer. It has been caught up and repeated, made the subject of acres of editorials, and hundreds if not thousands of cartoons, as if it were the last word upon the subject.

The usually dignified journals, which ordinarily display self-possession and intelligence in discussing public questions, have fallen at the feet of Mr. Havemeyer as a new prophet of economics. That the yellow journals, 16-to-1 advocates, populists and socialists, should make much of his utterance is not surprising, since they feed chiefly on the foam of sensation; but to find the sober papers and magazines vying with the gutter journals in this substitution of sensation for rational discussion indicates that the stream of public opinion is being polluted at its very source.

All this tends to show a dishonesty of utterance on public questions. The talk against great wealth by millionaire journalists like Bennett, Hearst and Pulitzer, capitalists like Havemeyer, and millionaire politicians like Alger and Pingree, of course is not to be taken seriously. They are performing to the galleries, they are catering to a public sentiment that has been created by systematic traducing of successful business men for political purposes. This is so general that frank, honest discussion of the public aspects of industry has become difficult and in many quarters impossible. Intellectual integrity in this field of public interests is rapidly being submerged and superseded by economic cant and public sensation. The extent to which this is taking place is painfully illustrated by the way in which the Havemeyer testimony is heralded and extolled by the press throughout the country.

From the homage paid him immediately after his testimony before the Industrial Commission, one might think that he was a statesman or economist whose opinions on important public questions should have great weight. Yet, really, he had never been suspected of anything of the kind. He has never said or done anything to entitle his opinion on matters of public concern to any special weight whatever. Mr. Havemeyer is known only as the president of the so-called "sugar trust," whose reputation is the most unsavory of any large industrial concern in this country. His trust has been notorious as a stock manipulator. It plays ducks and drakes with its own stock in the market place, making large profits out of unsuspecting investors. Under Mr. Havemeyer's leadership the sugar trust has been the most conspicuous as a manipulator of congress by doubtful methods. As recently as 1894, when the Wilson bill was before the United States senate, his trust was the most active factor in the lobby. He then believed that a high tariff was a very good thing, and labored long and hard to secure it for sugar. Indeed, his activity for high protection to sugar created a national scandal. Bold corruption and bribery were openly charged in the senate, and a committee was appointed to investigate the matter. At the hearing before this committee certain of Mr. Havemeyer's witnesses, conspicuous employees of the trust, were sent to jail for refusing to answer questions, which it was feared would have placed upon the sugar trust the crime of corrupting the United States senate. Nothing more scandalous has occurred in the public affairs of the republic.

At that time the free trade journals in the land furiously denounced Mr. Havemeyer as a low, selfish monopolist, a corrupter of legislators and a debaucher of public morals. His opinion on the tariff or any other public question was then regarded by the press as of no more account than the brawlings of a cheap politician or a cunning monopolist. Nothing has occurred since to indicate that Mr. Havemeyer is either more intelligent, more public-spirited or more honest now than he was in 1894. But now, when he appears before the Industrial Commission and declares that the tariff is the " mother of all trusts," his utterance is hailed as from one who speaks *ex cathedra*. If he believes that trusts are really a bad thing, then he is a disreputable man for being at the head of one. If he does not believe that, then he is a humbug for saying what he did. If trusts are legitimate and proper concerns, as he afterwards endeavored to show, then it would be nothing against the tariff if it were the mother of them all. It is a public benefit to be the mother of a good thing. The fact of the matter is that Mr. Havemeyer is neither honest enough, nor economist enough, nor public-spirited enough either to know or care whether trusts are good or bad, or whether they are helped or hindered by tariffs. His talk was illogical and contradictory and very clearly a case of " sour grapes " whining. Whatever may be the public interest in the case, Mr. Havemeyer's statement on the subject is utterly worthless, both from the moral and economic point of view. The only thing of significance in the Havemeyer situation is the fact that the press, after having treated him as a conscienceless corruptionist, should pretend to attach any importance to this obviously soured utterance. This fact is alike discreditable to the press and dangerous to the public sentiment of the nation.

But how much truth is there in Mr. Havemeyer's charge that: "The mother of all trusts is the customs tariff bill?" This is not a matter of opinion, but a question of fact, and it is the one statement in his address which is most heralded throughout the country. If Mr. Havemeyer is half as well informed on this point as those who are repeating his statement would have us believe, he knows that more than 90 per cent. of this statement is false. In the first place, there are practically no trusts in the country. Mr. Havemeyer knows that the American Sugar Refining Company, of which he is president, is not a trust. As a trust it was disorganized by law, and it is now simply a large corporation. The Standard Oil trust was the first, the largest and about the last trust, since it is just now about to be reorganized into a single corporation, just like any cotton or woolen or publishing corporation.

The tin-plate trust is due to the tariff only because the existence of the industry itself is due to protection. Before the tariff of 1890 there was no tin-plate manufactured in this country. The protection afforded by that measure made the investment of capital in the manufacture of tin-plate in this country possible. Through the use of modern methods and Yankee

14

industry, the American producers soon undersold the foreign producers and supplied the entire American market. As soon as it became an established industry, competition became sufficiently severe to reduce the price not only far below the foreign but below the profit-making point of all except a small proportion of the very best concerns. Reorganization for the sake of economy and efficiency became necessary in that industry as it has in hundreds of others, and in fact as it always does with industrial development. What were the plants of a number of tin-plate manufacturers are now the property of one corporation. As previously explained in this magazine,[1] although the price of tin-plate has been somewhat increased with the rise of wages and raw material, tin-plates are $1.10 a box less than when they were furnished, duty free, by English manufacturers.

The existence of the industry in this country was due to the protective tariff; but the reorganization of smaller concerns into a large one was due, not to the tariff, but to the competitive rivalry and needed economy in the business. There is no other industry in the country to which Havemeyer's statement is even approximately applicable. Take the great Carnegie concern, which is as much a trust as is the Standard Oil Company or the American Sugar Refining Company, or any other large corporation, called "trust," in the country. It is one of the largest iron and steel works in the world. It probably could not have come into existence if there had been no protective tariff for iron and steel, yet does Mr. Havemeyer or

---

[1] May number, 1899.

anybody else in his senses pretend to say that the Carnegie Company is a monster trust created by the tariff. The tariff gave the first stimulating opportunity to the iron and steel business, but Carnegie proved to be a superior industrial organizer. Under his leadership and management, the Carnegie corporation became a financial success. It acquired the leadership in its line in this country, and may ultimately in the whole world. It is now furnishing steel rails to foreign countries at a lower rate than the manufacturers of any other country.

The steam and surface railroad corporations and syndicates, large telegraph companies, colossal corporate concerns in every line of industry, are the result of one general cause, namely: the extraordinary industrial development of the country. Wherever industrial progress is rapid and permanent large enterprises arise, and conversely where industrial development is slow and meager, small individual concerns with restricted capital, primitive methods, high prices and low wages prevail. Hence large concerns are more numerous in the United States than anywhere else, and as industry develops they are making their appearance in England, France, Germany and other countries. The simple and well-nigh obvious fact is that large corporations follow business prosperity and progress, whether under protection or free trade. Whatever contributes to industrial development helps to build up large corporations, and whatever will destroy business prosperity will stop the growth of so-called trusts. To say that the tariff is the mother of trusts is to say that the tariff is the mother of business prosperity, which is not wholly without truth.

Witness the great surface railroad corporations in New York and other large cities throughout the country. They come the nearest to being monopolies of anything.in the land; they have given and are giving cheaper and better service than was ever before rendered to the public and are making immense profits, all of which is made possible by the general prosperity of the community, without which they would not have come into existence here any more than they have in China. Only to the extent that protection has promoted that prosperity has it helped to bring these great corporations into existence.

It is high time that at least the decent part of the American press awoke to the importance of infusing integrity and fairness into the discussion of public questions. The political and social integrity of the nation is far more important than any party success. No amount of political advantages can compensate for debauching public opinion, misleading and confusing the people on great industrial questions.

Tariffs and trusts should be discussed on their merits, separately. If large corporations are a menace to public welfare, let that fact be established by the data connected with corporate industry, and, if tariffs are a bad thing, let that be shown by the facts arising out of tariff legislation. But to confound the two when they have no necessary connection is demagogy, not discussion. To raise the alarm that large corporations are monopolies which oppress and rob the people, and in the same breath declare that protective tariffs are the cause of trusts, is at once to juggle with subjects and destroy popular confidence both in our political and industrial institutions.

XVI.

CRUSADE AGAINST PROSPERITY.*

THE United States in many respects is unique, but in nothing is it so strikingly different from all other countries as in the political attitude of the people towards business. It is a common occurrence in representative governments for the existing ministry to be defeated through the influence of hard times. Disraeli once said that no English ministry could withstand three bad harvests. But a very poor ministry can keep power with good times. This tendency to make political confidence depend chiefly on business prosperity prevails in every country except the United States.

By some peculiarity of temperament or psychological influence the people of the United States seem to delight in using their political power against business development and prosperity. Several times in the midst of prosperity a political movement has arisen demanding a radical change in the fiscal or tariff policy, resulting in the destruction of business confidence, paralysis of industry, and sometimes a financial panic, —witness 1892–93. As the result of that we had six years of business depression and social hardship. Now, under a return to the former policy, business confidence and prosperity have returned,—and we are getting

---

* Published in *Gunton's Magazine* of September 1899.

ready to destroy it again. In 1892 the means of attacking business prosperity was the overthrow of the tariff, now it is the overthrow of corporations. The war cry is being raised from one end of the land to the other: " Down with trusts."

This is not merely the work of a few crank reformers and irresponsible agitators, but it is being made the issue of a systematized political campaign, supported by numerous independent movements. Indeed, it almost seems as if the American people would soon be as mad on the trust question as the French people are on the Dreyfus question.

If this movement against trusts is to take on a practical form, in common justice to the people the object should be frankly presented. Suppose the forthcoming conference of governors is a success and all the states act together, what is to be accomplished? Of course the talk is that this great national uprising is to abolish trusts. But suppose there are no trusts. What then? The army has been organized, the guns are loaded, and somebody must be killed to justify the effort. If there are no trusts, then of course an attack must be made upon corporations.

Now that is exactly the state of the case. There is not a trust in the United States. There never were more than about half a dozen, and they have all been dissolved and converted into large corporations. In reality, then, the war on trusts is a war on corporations pure and simple. Large corporations may be a very bad thing for the community, and if so they ought to be abolished, but an agitation for their abolition should be conducted on honest principles. It should be definitely understood that it is a crusade against large corporations. To call it a crusade against trusts is to practise a fraud upon the people. At least let us have the people who are to vote these business concerns out of existence know what they are voting against. Certainly before the people of this country can be expected to support such a crusade they have a right to know something about what it will accomplish.

First, then, are all corporations to be suppressed? If so the proposition is very simple. Of course this can be done if the people want it, but it would stop every railroad, trolley, cable and horse-car system in the country, and would close more than ninety per cent. of the manufacturing and business concerns. In fact, nearly all businesses larger than the peanut stand would have to be dissolved and re-distributed into small efforts, about the equivalent of what existed in the walled towns in the thirteenth century. It would, in fact, wipe out about all the economic effectiveness the last five centuries of industrial evolution have produced. For reduction to economic simplicity and thorough abolition of monopoly this would leave little to be desired. It would accomplish the object completely, but it would reduce us to barbarism. Of course nobody wants that.

Yet that is the simple case if the war is against all corporations. If it is not against all corporations, then against which is the war to be directed? If we are not to suppress all, there must be some specific line of distinction between those " to be damned " and those " to be saved." There must be some way of distinguishing the sheep from the goats. What shall it be? It cannot be anything relating to the economic or political principle of the organization, because in these respects they are all alike. Nor is it in the character of the industry, because the corporation principle applies to all industries. There is only one difference between them and that is the size of their capital. Well, then, where shall the line be drawn? Shall it be at one hundred thousand, at half a million, a million, five millions, ten millions, fifty millions or a hundred millions? Where? If the line is to be drawn anywhere, some economic or political reason must be given for drawing it there. Upon what economic principle or experience can a distinction be made? Some of the economists who are to address the Chicago conference or the governors who are to enlighten the St. Louis conference are in honor bound to give this information to the people, or else abandon their movement. If there is any reason, economic, moral or political, why a corporation of half a million capital is a good thing and one with a million or five millions capital is bad, then a benighted world is waiting for the information. Thus far not a ray of light has ever been shed upon that point, though acres of literature on the subject have been published.

How came these corporations to get so large? Why did they organize at all? There is one general reason and it is this: in the effort to make the most of invested capital, it was found by a long series of experiments that under certain conditions large capital could be used to greater advantage than small capital; it could produce more at the same cost, give a larger profit, sell the products at lower prices, and give more permanent employment to labor at higher wages. Every little addition to the size of industrial concerns has been made for these reasons. As the experiments

proved a success they were increased, and so from
small individual concerns to partnerships and corporations the process went on and on, and if not arbitrarily interrupted will continue to go on just so long as
it will yield these advantages.   Just so long as adding
another million to the plant will increase the earning
capacity of both the old and new capital, the additions
will continue to be made, and as soon as the point is
reached where to increase the size only increases the
unwieldiness and does not increase the economy it will
stop.

Clearly, then, the history of industrial growth and
prosperity is the history of corporate development.
Without corporations productive efficiency could not
have progressed beyond the economic status of the
small individual concerns of at least a century ago.   A
war on corporations, without some definite economic
basis of discrimination, then, is simply a war on business success.   That is the character of the present
movement.   It is based upon no principle of industrial
management or public policy.   It recognizes no line of
distinction between the good and the bad, but it is a
blind, muddled, indiscriminate agitation against corporate capital, which means a crusade against business
prosperity.

What would be accomplished if this crusade against
corporations should succeed?   A few instances serve
to illustrate what might be expected.   Take, for instance, the Standard Oil Company, which is constantly
cited as a conspicuous object of attack.   The petroleum
industry began in 1859.   From then until about 1871
illuminating oil was produced by a large number of
small concerns.   The oil was very poor and dangerous

to use. From 1863 inclusive, when oil production was becoming an established business and full statistics are available, until 1871, the gold price fell from $30\frac{7}{10}$ cents to $21\frac{7}{10}$ cents per gallon, or $29\frac{3}{10}$ per cent. From 1871 to 1880, under the Standard Oil Company, the price fell from $21\frac{7}{10}$ to $9\frac{1}{8}$ cents, or 58 per cent., and under the " trust " it has fallen from $9\frac{1}{8}$ to $5\frac{7}{10}$ cents, or $37\frac{5}{10}$ per cent. The average yearly prices in gold for the whole period from 1861 to 1898 are as follows:

Year	Average Yearly Price (Cents)	Year	Average Yearly Price (Cents)
1863	$30\frac{7}{10}$	1881	8
1864	$31\frac{1}{5}$	1882	$7\frac{3}{8}$
1865	$37\frac{3}{10}$	1883	$8\frac{1}{8}$
1866	$30\frac{1}{10}$	1884	$8\frac{1}{4}$
1867	$20\frac{1}{2}$	1885	$8\frac{1}{4}$
1868	$20\frac{3}{4}$	1886	$7\frac{1}{4}$
1869	$24\frac{3}{5}$	1887	$6\frac{3}{4}$
1870	$22\frac{9}{10}$	1888	$7\frac{1}{4}$
1871	$21\frac{7}{10}$	1889	$7\frac{1}{4}$
1872	21	1890	$7\frac{3}{4}$
1873	16	1891	$6\frac{9}{10}$
1874	$11\frac{7}{10}$	1892	$6\frac{7}{10}$
1875	$11\frac{3}{10}$	1893	$5\frac{1}{4}$
1876	$17\frac{1}{10}$	1894	$5\frac{1}{8}$
1877	15	1895	$7\frac{1}{8}$
1878	$10\frac{3}{5}$	1896	7
1879	$8\frac{1}{4}$	1897	$5\frac{9}{10}$
1880	$9\frac{1}{8}$	1898	$5\frac{7}{10}$

This immense reduction of the price, besides improvement of the quality, has been accomplished by no aid of legislation, but by the economic use of capital and unlimited scientific experiment in the process of refining and handling the oil. This would have been impossible by any small capital. The pipe line itself could not have been built by individual effort or anything short of a colossal organization. By the increase of capital and development of new devices this concern has developed an enormous industry; from a product in 1859 of 9,500 barrels to 35,165,990 barrels in 1897.

In the early seventies petroleum was discovered in Russia, and when the Standard Oil Company made its great improvements in the methods and processes of refining and completed its pipe-line transportation, at an outlay of millions of dollars in experimentation and construction, European capital organized an immense syndicate and adopted all the improved methods of the Standard Oil Company in developing the oil industry in Russia. They have increased the Russian production from 100,000 barrels in 1870 to 50,697,000 barrels in 1897, which is 15,531,010 barrels more than the total American output. The record of Russia's oil production by years, since 1870, is follows :

Year	Barrels	Year	Barrels
1870	100,000	1884	8,841,000
1871	150,000	1885	11,894,000
1872	175,000	1886	14,784,000
1873	250,000	1887	16,208,000
1874	500,000	1888	18,860,000
1875	750,000	1889	20,137,000
1876	1,000,000	1890	23,477,000
1877	1,250,000	1891	28,290,000
1878	2,000,000	1892	29,273,000
1879	2,250,000	1893	33,104,000
1880	2,455,000	1894	30,383,000
1881	3,920,000	1895	38,340,000
1882	4,911,000	1896	46,352,000
1883	5,893,000	1897	50,697,000

Thus, with the best American methods, developed at the cost of the experiments of American capital, and paying less than one-fourth American wages, and with the most fertile oil lands in the world, Russia has become an immense rival in the petroleum industry. The Russian government protects the Russian market by a 200 per cent. duty, so that the Russian oil company has a monopoly of the Russian market. It has cheap labor and American productive methods to compete against the Standard Oil Company in the rest of the world.

On the other hand, by its superior economy, large capital and highly developed management, the Standard Oil Company has prevented Russian oil producers from supplying the American market. By the use of immense capital and efficient management the American producers, besides supplying the American market, in 1897 exported to the different countries of Europe, Asia and elsewhere, outside of Russia, 994,297,757 gallons of refined oil, which, at the low prevailing price, was equivalent to bringing $59,057,574 in gold into the country. The exports for the last ten years have been as follows:

Year	Gallons	Dollars	Year	Gallons	Dollars
1888	572,457,975	48,105,703	1893	871,757,017	41,117,814
1889	680,705,456	53,293,299	1894	894,162,155	40,483,088
1890	693,829,848	52,270,953	1895	853,126,130	56,228,425
1891	673,905,577	46,174,835	1896	931,785,022	62,764,278
1892	744,638,463	42,729,157	1897	994,297,757	59,057,547

Here, then, is a concern which, by the power of its large capital, gives employment to 35,000 American laborers, pays $100,000 a day in wages, and brings nearly $60,000,000 of gold into the country every year; which would be lost to this country but for the economic energy and superiority of the Standard Oil Company. Who would be benefited if this concern were forced to disband? Small refineries, such as those now outside the Standard, could not even hold the American market, if subjected to competition with the Russians.   Moreover, the Standard Oil Company furnishes an unlimited cash market for every barrel of petroleum produced in this country.

Take the railroads as another instance.   Next to the Standard Oil Company probably the railroads are the most conspicuous objects of attack by this new crusade.   If the recommendations of Mr. Cleveland in his last message, and the program of the coming conference of governors in St. Louis, are to be consummated, then the great railroad corporations must be broken up, or confiscated by the government, which is what the socialist part of the movement most desires and really hopes for.

In 1873, with the relatively small and unintegrated railroad corporations, it cost 2.21 cents a mile to ship a ton of merchandise.   By the steady enlargement of systems and economizing of costs, without lowering but in many instances raising wages, the freight charge has been gradually lowered from 2.21 cents a mile in 1873 to about .75 of a cent a mile in 1898, a fall of about 64 per cent., as will be seen by the following table :

Years	Miles of Railroad	Average rate per ton per mile (cents)	Years	Miles of Railroad	Average rate per ton per mile (cents)
1873	70,268	2.210	1886	136,379	1.042
1874	72,385	2.040	1887	149,257	1.034
1875	74,096	1.810	1888	156,169	0.977
1876	76,808	1.855	1889	161,353	0.970
1877	79,088	1.524	1890	166,698	0.997
1878	81,767	1.401	1891	170,769	0.929
1879	86,584	1.201	1892	175,188	0.941
1880	93,296	1.348	1893	177,465	0.893
1881	103,143	1.264	1894	179,393	0.864
1882	114,712	1.236	1895	181,021	0.839
1883	121,455	1.224	1896	182,777	0.806
1884	125,379	1.125	1897	184,428	0.798
1885	128,361	1.036	1898	186,396	0.753

It will be seen that during the last twenty-four years, in which the railroads have developed into larger and larger corporations, the cost of service to the public has been lessened more than one half, to say nothing of the immensely improved passenger service facilities and smoother roadbeds.

The simple English of these facts is that to resolve the railroad corporations back, even into the original small concerns, which were corporations, would probably be to more than double the cost of railroad service to the people. Who would be benefited by such a performance? It would be a setback of a quarter of a century, with an injury to everybody and benefit to nobody. Are the American people ready for any such retrogressive folly?

Next to the steam railroad corporations, those most railed against are the surface railroad system syndicates, especially those which control the surface railroad systems in our large cities. Take New York as an example. All the surface railroading in New York city is in the hands of two companies. It was once in the hands of a dozen or more companies. Every avenue line and every crosstown line was run by a separate company. Under that régime the motive power was horses, and the public had to pay a separate five-cent fare for every car boarded. With the discovery of new motive power, trolleys, cable and lastly under-ground-conduit trolleys, larger capital was needed to get the best effects from the new methods, and to-day the citizens of New York (and by the same process of nearly all the cities in the country) can ride in cars many times as commodious and wholesome, twice as fast, ten times as far, and be transferred to numerous other lines, all for one fare. Under this system of concentrated capital and management citizens of New York can now board a trolley on the New York side of Brooklyn Bridge, cross the bridge and ride some dozen miles to Coney Island, for five cents, which formerly by any other route cost 40 and 50 cents. By an agreement between the Third Avenue Company and elevated road system, which is practically another large integration, passengers can travel from the Battery to New Rochelle, a distance of twenty-five miles or more, for eight cents,—a five-cent fare and a three-cent transfer,—which by the steam railroads costs about 40 cents.

The next natural step, one that will come if not arbitrarily interfered with, will be to put the entire local transit system of the metropolis, both surface and elevated, under one management. Then every road in every direction will be open to the public for a single fare, transfers being accepted from any to any other cars in the entire city. What will the new crusade do with this?

If its policy is to be carried out the great meat-packing establishments of Chicago, the steel manufacturing corporations of Pittsburg, will have to be disbanded and industry relegated back to the primitive methods existing in the ante-corporation period. This would practically mean an increase of from 50 to 100 per cent. in the price of nearly all machine made products.

Of course it will be said that this is not what is intended, but what has already been done justifies the belief that the madness will, if it can, go to the full length. Take for example the state of Ohio. It has practically legislated the Standard Oil Company out of the state. Through a system of legal persecution, doing business in Ohio has been made intolerable and the works which employed thousands of men and distributed hundreds of thousands of dollars a year in Cleveland and other cities in that state are being closed and removed. It will not take much of this to bring the people of Ohio to a realizing sense of the economic madness of this policy.

In Michigan also the work goes bravely on, but in even greater degree. A law was passed recently, under Governor Pingree's influence, making it a misdemeanor to make a contract affecting the price of any commodity for future delivery. The law says:

"It shall hereafter be unlawful for two or more persons to make or enter into or execute or carry out any contracts or obligations or agreements by which they shall bind themselves to sell any commodity between them so as to directly or indirectly preclude a free and unrestricted competition among themselves."

The penalty for violating this law is a fine of from $50.00 to $5,000.00, or imprisonment for a term of six months to one year, or both. Now, if a person cannot enter into or carry out any contract or agreement binding himself to sell a commodity at a special price for any time in the future, then there is no freedom of contract whatever. Not a single large industry could be conducted successfully under such a law. It would be the entire suppression of modern methods of business.

The legislators of Texas and Kentucky and other states are vying with each other as to which can pass the most effective business-killing legislation. The more this anti-trust movement is considered in the light of its own declarations and accomplishments, in the light of logic, common sense and economic sanity, the clearer it becomes that it is a fanatical, misguided crusade against business prosperity, public welfare and national progress.

XVII

FROM THE PUBLIC POINT OF VIEW *

THE trust question is only a new phase of an old problem—the problem of free industrial enterprise. Notwithstanding the well-known fact that the marvelous progress of the last three-quarters of a century is mainly due to the introduction of improved methods of industry, every improvement since Wyatt's spinning frame and Hargreaves' spinning jenny has had to fight its way against the popular prejudice of the time. The hand-loom weavers marched through England and broke the power looms. Hargreaves, Arkwright and Crompton were driven from their homes for inventing new methods of spinning.

Now, after three-quarters of a century's experience, in which the fallacy of this policy has become notorious, we are face to face with another movement of the same character. The present agitation against trusts has all the characteristics of the anti-machinery riots of a century ago. It pervades the attitude of both laborers and business men alike. Workingmen give about the same reasons for opposing the introduction of new machines as did the neighbors of Crompton and Arkwright for breaking their spinning frames. The business men who twenty-five years ago were among the

* Address delivered at the Chicago trust conference, September 14, 1899.

226

hated organizers of corporations are now among the agitators against trusts. And now the movement is taking on a political form. Men of national repute, and leaders of great political parties, candidates for the highest and most responsible positions in the nation, are asking the people to reverse the policy of industrial freedom and return to the doctrine of arbitrary paternalism, specifically to suppress large corporations. Are the American people ready for such a step?

There is only one point of view from which this subject can properly be considered—the interest of the public; the public as representing the consumers who are interested in superior commodities at low prices; the public as representing the laborers who are interested in permanent employment and good wages; the public as representing the farmers who are interested in cheap transportation and the advantages of the modern products of science, art and literature. It is in these aspects of the subject, and not in the confusing clamor and sensational subterfuge of campaign oratory, that the American people are interested. The question for this conference to ask, the question for the people of the United States to ask, is: Are trusts inimical to public welfare in all or any of these respects?

It must be remembered, first of all, that the trust, be it good or bad, is only one among a large number of experiments in industrial organization, which the progress of the last fifty years has evolved. One of the marked features of the economic development of the century is the radical change that has taken place in the character of competing units. Under the primitive hand labor method, the competing unit was the individual. With the development of factory methods, the individual as a competing unit was superseded by partnerships, because they could more economically employ the new methods. With the growth of invention, partnerships were superseded by corporations. With the growing completeness of machinery and magnitude of business, corporations grew larger and larger, until the corporation is now the prevailing industrial form in the most advanced countries.

Nor is this limited to the capitalist side of industry. It is equally characteristic of the labor side. The competing unit in the labor market is no longer the individual laborer, but the group, the union. The factory system has made it impossible for individual laborers to be competitors, because it is impossible for them to make individual contracts. In all matters pertaining to wages, hours of labor, conditions of work, whether by piece or by the day, it is the group and not the individual that is considered. Each factory, and in most instances each industry, pays uniform wages, works the same hours, and has substantially the same conditions, and when they are altered for one they are altered for all. In short, the progress during the nineteenth century has irrevocably established the group as the competing unit; the union as the unit on the labor side, the corporation as the unit on the capital side.

Now, the trust was one of the experiments in the evolution of this group unit. Numerous forms of organization and association were tried. Corners, associations to fix prices, were tried; but these were uneconomic and failed, usually wrecking somebody in the collapse. The trust was another form. It differed from these in that it was an attempt to integrate productive forces. Corners and trade associations were mere manipulators of prices, not producers. Trusts were *bona fide* producers.

The difference between the trust and the ordinary corporations is not economic, but legal. The trusts are a formal merging of a number of corporations or firms under one management, which holds the property in trust for its original owners, giving certificates for their respective claims. There have been very few *bona fide* trusts; the Standard Oil trust, the sugar trust and a few others. But, through the intense popular opposition, resulting in adverse legislation, these have all disappeared. They have been disbanded and converted into simple corporations, with capital stock owned by whomsoever chooses to invest, and governed by the majority vote of the stockholders. So that, if there was anything peculiar or alarming in trusts, the evil has disappeared, because the trust is gone.

In reality, then, what we have are simply corporations. The whole question which this conference is called to consider is: what is the influence of large corporations upon public welfare?

First, then, what is the effect of large corporations upon the quality and price of the community's supply of commodities? This question is one of fact, and can be adequately answered only by experience. The history of corporations on this point is almost too obvious to need reciting. The evidence abounds on every hand. While experience differs in different industries, as it necessarily must, the tendency is universal that with the growth of large corporations the quality of the commodities improves, and the prices fall. It was in obedience to this principle that corporations came into existence. A long series of experiments taught that under certain conditions large capital could be used to greater advantage than small capital. It could produce more at the same cost, give a larger aggregate profit, by selling the products at lower prices. As the experiments proved successful they were increased, and so from small individual concerns to partnerships, then to corporations, the process went on and on, and if not arbitrarily interrupted will continue to go on just so long as it will yield any advantage. Just so long as adding another million to the plant will increase the earning capacity of both the old and new capital, the additions will continue to be made, and as soon as the point is reached where to increase the size fails to increase the economy, it will stop. Clearly, the history of industrial growth and prosperity is the history of corporate development. Without corporations productive efficiency could not have progressed beyond the economic status of the small individual concerns of the last century.

The era of corporations in this country is since the war. It is during that period that our industrial expansion has been so enormous and the great corporate interests have developed. Prices of the leading manufactured products, mostly produced by corporations, and some of them by very large corporations, using most modern machinery, have fallen varying from 6 to 40 per cent. At the same time wages have risen, chiefly in the manufacturing and mercantile industries, 68 per cent.

While this is true of corporate industries in general, as compared with non-corporate industries, it is most markedly true of very large corporations. If we take the concerns where millions are invested by a single corporation, like the Standard Oil Company, the American Sugar Refining Company, the great rail-roads, the Carnegie Steel Company, we find that their products have undergone the greatest improvement in quality and the greatest reduction in price. Without the immensely large capitals invested by these great corporations, many of the great improvements accomplished during the last twenty years would have been absolutely impossible. Take for instance the Carnegie Company. Nothing short of tens of millions invested under one management could have developed the extraordinary improvements which have revolutionized both the quality and price of iron and steel products. With small concerns of less than a million each, that could not have been done. The same is true of our great railroad systems. No small or individual enterprise could have given us the marvelous development in railroading of the last twenty-five years, which has constantly improved the service and so greatly reduced the cost to the public. In 1873 it cost 2.21 cents a mile to transport a ton of freight. Through the increased investments and improved facilities, the price has been gradually reduced year by year until now it only costs 75-hundredths of a cent a mile per ton. The surface railroad systems throughout this country are another illustration of what large corporations can and do accomplish. It used to cost ten cents to ride a few blocks in a dingy, dirty horse car, in any city in this country. With the development of large corporations, electricity has superseded horses; large, light and wholesome cars have replaced dingy boxes, and fares have been reduced one-half, with transfers to nearly all connecting lines, a result that could not have been accomplished under small separate concerns.

Next, what is the influence of corporations upon the conditions of labor? It is commonly asserted that large corporations tend to destroy the laborer's liberty and individuality by making him a part of a productive machine. Mr. Cleveland sounded this note in his last message to congress. A little touch of fact would show this to be a pure phantom of the imagination. Nothing could be more contrary to the whole history of wage labor. If there were any truth in this, we might expect to find that laborers had more freedom and greater individuality before the wage system began. Yet everybody knows that then they had neither liberty nor individuality; that it was not until long after the wage system came that laborers acquired any liberty, political rights or social individuality. ·

The laborer's freedom and individuality depend upon two things—permanence of employment and good wages. Wherever the employment of labor is most permanent and wages are highest, there the laborer is most intelligent, has the greatest freedom and the strongest individual identity. Where do laborers get these conditions? It is not where capital is small and employers are poor. On the contrary, it is where large corporations prevail that wages are highest and employment most continuous, and everybody knows it is there where the laborers are most independent. It is notorious that large corporations have the least influence over the opinions and individual conduct of their laborers.   Let it be known that a large corpora-tion is trying to influence the election of candidates for office, and that is the signal for the working men to vote against them.   Instead of being controlled by the corporations they act almost uniformly on the rule of defying and opposing them.

Nor is there any loss of individual liberty in becom-ing a fractional part of a large productive concern. What society wants is not individuality as producers but individuality as citizens.   What we need is that the laborer should give less and less of his personal energy to earning a living and more and more to his social and individual improvement.   A permanent stipulated in-come is the first step towards real individual freedom for the laborers.   Nothing is so depressing to man-hood, nothing makes the weak so cowardly, as pre-cariousness of income.   The small business man who does not know from quarter to quarter, and sometimes from month to month, whether he can meet his obli-gations, is neither so brave, so intelligent nor so free a citizen as the wage laborer in the safe employ of a large corporation.   As a matter of fact, the corpora-tion and banker have far more influence over the votes of small business men whom they have befriended or patronized than they have over their own laborers. A laborer's freedom does not depend upon the fact that he works for wages, but on the amount of his wages.   With high wages and permanent employment the laborer's freedom and welfare are secured.   The laborer has not a single interest, social, economic or political, in the existence of employers with small capital.

How do large corporations affect the interest of the farmers? There is probably no class in the community who derive more benefit from the economic improvements of large corporations than the farmers. All the great improvements in tools, architecture, sanitation, domestic appointments, art, literature and general refinements are the products of industrial centers where large capitalistic enterprises abound. Every form of commodity outside of food which enters into the farmer's life has been immensely improved and greatly cheapened by the efforts of large corporations. Transportation, which is an important item in the farmer's economy, has been reduced 50 per cent. during the last twenty-five years. While the farmer has received all the advantages produced by large corporations in lower prices of everything he buys, and lower transportation, the price of what he sells has undergone very little fall; many of than no fall at all, and some have even risen.

What is the influence of large corporations upon business stability and prosperity? This is one of the most important features of the subject. The greatest menace to modern society is business depressions, which usually are the result of ignorant eagerness among competitors. A slight boom in business leads to a rash increase of output. Without any general knowledge of what is being done elsewhere, each hopes to fill the new void, with the result of an increase of output wholly disproportionate to the demand. For instance, the Illinois farmer, when the price of corn is high, will double his acreage for corn, and next year finds that he can hardly sell the corn at any price, and is compelled to use it for fuel. Large concerns tend to remedy this evil on the same principle that they invest heavily in experimentation. They take pains to gather accurate information of the condition of their business throughout the world. They find it pays to be informed as to what next year's demand is likely to be. Their investments are so large that they could not afford seriously to miscalculate the demands of the market. With their comparatively accurate information, they adjust their production with great precision to the present and probable future demand. As a matter of fact, in lines of industry where the very largest concerns are organized there is the least perturbation. If the raising of corn were in the hands of a few well-informed corporations instead of thousands of uninformed small farmers, the erratic ups and downs in corn-farming would be largely avoided. Industrial depressions can never be eliminated until the relation of productive enterprise to general consumption is reduced to some degree of precision, which the small go-as-you-please producers can never do.

Large corporations are superior to small concerns; first, because by the use of large capital and superior methods they improve the quality and reduce the price of commodities; second, they are more favorable than smaller concerns to high wages, and individual freedom of laborers; third, by introducing scientific precision into industry they tend to increase the permanence of employment and reduce the tendency to industrial depressions, all of which are vital elements in the nation's prosperity and progress.

In studying the literature against large corporations one is impressed by the marked absence of careful presentation of facts and rational discussion of the case. There seems to be no attempt to apply economic principles or recognize the great law of societary evolution. The only hint thus far of a policy to be adopted is the proposition of Mr. Bryan, which is that congress pass a law forbidding all corporations to do business outside the state in which they are incorporated without a license from the federal government. It is difficult to imagine a gentleman, who is about to be for the second time a candidate for the presidency of the United States, seriously making such a proposition. This is so contrary to the spirit and traditions of democracy, which is usually opposed to any trade restrictions whatever, and so contrary to the American idea of free intercourse between the states, and so contrary to Mr. Bryan's previous declarations, that one has difficulty in taking him seriously. If this is really the best that his mind can suggest on the subject, it is a depressing gauge of his statesmanship. It would hardly be possible to invent a proposition that would be more fertile in creating corruption, injustice, favoritism and business demoralization. A license might be granted by one administration and refused by another, for purely political reasons, which would be equal to confiscating the property of the corporation, since it would destroy its business value. There is not a single aspect of this proposition which is not surcharged with economic and political iniquity. It partakes neither of economic sense, political wisdom, fair statesmanship, nor even party shrewdness.

It is not to be assumed, however, that large corporations are always wise, or good, or fair. They are born of the same spirit and partake of the same attributes as small business venders. Their main ambition

is to make profits. It is the duty of the state, therefore, to see to it that the conditions shall be such as to
make dishonesty, unfairness, oppressive dealing, difficult and as impossible as any other offenses against
the welfare of the community.   This cannot be accomplished, however, by the petty nagging and corrup-
tion-creating, license-granting scheme proposed by Mr.
Bryan.   The Federal government if it acts at all should
act in exactly the other direction.   It should surround
industrial enterprise with the maximum freedom and
protection to all, and no economic privilege to any.

To this end it might be well for congress to enact a
law empowering the government to grant national
charters to corporations, which should give them the
right to do business over the entire territory of the and
United States, and against which no state should have
the right to interfere.   This would be economic, in that
it would give the market of the entire country to every
business enterprise.   National charters could have
the proper qualifications subjecting the corporations
to a certain supervision and compelling annual reports
to be made.   Second, it might also be provided that
companies using a public franchise, like railroads, should
not be permitted to make economic discriminations in
their rates of traffic, that they should be subject to public accounting, and that all contracts with shippers
should be accessible to all other shippers.   The general
influence of publicity and inspection by the national
government, coupled with the corporation's protection
in its right to do business throughout the United States,
would tend to create a wholesome influence around
corporate conduct.   While affording corporations the
full support of the national government in their busi-

ness rights, it would free them from the petty uneconomic nagging of partisan legislation in the different states. It would carry out the true idea of protection —that the American market should be open to every American producer and that the interests of the laborers and the public be safeguarded by the national government; at the same time leaving the essential features of business to be determined by the free action of economic forces, which are more permanent, more sure and more equitable, than the wisest statutory enactment ever would be.

INDEX

16

www.ingramcontent.com/pod-product-compliance
Lightning Source LLC
Chambersburg PA
CBHW030801020726
47499CB00006B/1724